Watchmen of Asteri Series

Book One

Mia Johnson

~ Diviney family
God bless!

~Mia Johnson

Mia L. Johnson

Disclaimer: This book is a work of fiction. Any similarities to real people and places is not intended.

Copyright ©*2023 Mia L. Johnson*

Published by Mia Johnson.

All rights reserved. No part of this book may be reproduced, or any derivative work produced in any form, including, but not limited to, photocopying, recording, taping, word processing, scanning, or by any information storage retrieval system, without permission of the author, except as permitted by the U.S. copyright law.

ISBN: 979-8-9875911-0-9 (paperback)

Scripture quotations taken from the (NASB®) New American Standard Bible®, Copyright © 1960, 1971 by The Lockman Foundation. Used by permission. All rights reserved. www.lockman.org

Proverbs 12:22
Ecclesiastes 3:4
John 3:16-17

Printed in the United States of America

This book is dedicated to my parents and siblings, who supported and encouraged me in every way. But more importantly, this book is dedicated to the Lord over all things, God Most High.

Mia L. Johnson

Contents

1. Chapter One 7
2. Chapter Two 17
3. Chapter Three 26
4. Chapter Four 34
5. Chapter Five 41
6. Chapter Six 55
7. Chapter Seven 65
8. Chapter Eight 77
9. Chapter Nine 85
10. Chapter Ten 97
11. Chapter Eleven 108
12. Chapter Twelve 118
13. Chapter Thirteen 126
14. Chapter Fourteen 138
15. Chapter Fifteen 150
16. Chapter Sixteen 160
17. Chapter Seventeen 169
18. Chapter Eighteen 178
19. Chapter Nineteen 187
Characters 197
Acknowledgments 199
Author's Note 201

Mia L. Johnson

Chapter One

Vela couldn't wait to get onto land for once in her life. Last time the ship had anchored in this bay, she had made a friend her own age. She imagined sitting on the docks fishing or running through a green pasture. Nobody yelling at her, no ropes to jump over, and where the ground stayed in one place.

"Enemy ship off the starboard bow!"

The cry jolted Vela out of her daydreaming. With long bounds, the lithe girl scurried up to the top deck, where her trainer, the ship's captain, was standing.

A light sea breeze ruffled Vela's golden-brown hair, just as it had for the many past years. Her training as part of the Sails—a team under the larger group of the Watchmen of Asteri—had caused her to quickly advance her skills, and for a good reason. The Sails, with their small ships built for speed and agility, guarded the ocean border of Asteri.

"What country is it from, Captain?" Vela asked as she scrambled up the steep ladder.

"It's a Mevolen warship," Muhif's rumbling deep voice answered. He was a big man with black hair and a ragged beard.

I wonder if he really does cut his beard with his long knife as the crew claims, Vela wondered, not for the first time. But she never said anything aloud.

Neither did anyone else dare to. Nobody except the Watchman Commodore Louris and the king would tell Captain Muhif what to do.

He held out the spyglass. "What do you think our options are?"

Recognizing Muhif's question as another part of her training, Vela put the glass up to one of her green eyes. She pondered then said, "Well, if we give chase that might be what they're wanting us to do to draw us into a trap. So, if we stay here for another day before going into port, we might discourage them from coming any closer." Lowering the glass, she looked at the captain. "As long as they don't come nearer by nightfall, then I think we're good."

Muhif nodded. "Go see if the cook has enough food to last us till tomorrow."

Vela snapped a salute. "Aye aye, sir."

A thrill of exhilaration shot through Vela as she skimmed down the ladder. Muhif was training her to command her own ship someday. *Command my own ship!*

True, the ships held a crew of only about ten men not including the cook, but that was all the small ship needed. Just twenty meters in length, the Watchmen ships were not the biggest or most impressive boats on the sea, but they served their purpose. The *Eling's* bow was smooth and cut through the water almost without a splash. The pure white sails billowed and filled with wind, sending the ship slicing across the waves.

Vela landed lightly and walked across the swaying deck to the hatch. She opened it and scrambled down another ladder before entering a low doorway to the left of the ladder. This opening led to the ship's galley.

The galley was only ten feet square. A large table in the center took up most of the space. As always, it was cluttered with bowls, mixing spoons, and a pot. A box of dried meat sat next to the workbench.

In one corner, a box of sand held a dying fire, while a cauldron hung a half a foot above the embers. The sand kept the coals off the wooden deck boards. Even the greenest sailor knew that a cooking fire could quickly turn a wooden ship into a pile of charred planks and ashes.

"Cook?" Vela called into the galley.

A roundish man wearing a stained white apron popped up from behind a wooden counter. He smiled, showing a mouth full of teeth as stained as his apron.

"Hallo, Vela. Have ye come to help ole Cook in the kitchen today?"

"No, at least not right now. Muhif asked me to check if we have enough food to last us till tomorrow. He sighted a Mevolen warship and wants to make sure it's not going to slip past us."

"So that's whit all the commotion was about up thar." Cook nodded his head up and down, much like what a turkey would do. He checked the storage room ledger hanging on the wall. "Aye, we have plenty." Then he asked, "Are ye lookin forward to visitin' the mainland?"

"You know I am." Vela smiled as she remembered all the conversations she had with Cook. "I need to go report to Muhif now. Bye!"

She waved at Cook then ran out the door and back the way she'd come, easily threading through the sailors. As Vela skipped around one of the men who doubled as a warrior, she pitied any Mevolens who went up against these well-trained soldiers.

Skidding to a stop next to Muhif, Vela reported what she had learned, "Cook says we have plenty of food. Anything else you need?"

Muhif shook his head, appearing deep in thought.

A sailor called to Vela just then. "Want to take a watch in the Fighter's Top?"

Agreeing readily, Vela sprang into the rigging like one of those foreign monkeys she had seen on the Jelinian ships that sometimes stopped at port.

Making her way through the maze of ropes to the lookout post was no great challenge. Vela had been sailing since her childhood. Her father, a successful merchant, had always taken his family with him on his travels.

A few years later, at age sixteen, Vela apprenticed herself to Muhif in order to protect her country by guarding the sea from marauding pirates and enemy ships.

Now, two years later, Vela had no regrets. *I'm still in love with the sea.*

Every time she came up here, her breath was taken away even after years of traversing the seas. Crystal clear water as far as her eye could see surrounded her on three sides. A dark strip of land appeared on the last side.

Leaning on the railing surrounding the Fighter's Top, Vela watched the enemy ship grow smaller as the light began to fade. She stayed up a little longer to watch the sun set. The colors reflected off the water like a mirror reflected her face.

First it glowed bright yellow, then fiery orange, blood red, and finally midnight blue.

Vela toyed with a small anchor on a light chain around her neck. It was the custom in those days for the apprentices to wear their emblems in silver until they graduated. After graduation the apprentices could have their pendants in gold.

During the peaceful scene, Cook rang the bell summoning the first half of sailors to supper. Vela knew she should climb down to eat, so she grabbed a loose rope and slid down. Her feet pinched the rope to control her downward movement.

Vela landed right on time to see half of the sailors stream toward the sleeping quarters where they would eat their supper. Grabbing a plate of salted beef and a biscuit, she ate fast.

The prospect of being on land tomorrow cheered the crew and the banter between many of the men was low and common. "I don't want to get caught up in one of their jokes again," she muttered around a bite of biscuit. Then she sighed. "Aye, not again." Being the only lady on the ship, plenty of pranks were thrown her way, but the men also respected her. *As they should!*

Even in the pitch dark, Vela could find her way to the small room next to the captain's quarters. She crawled into her hammock, pulled the blanket up, and fell fast asleep, rocked by the ocean's gentle waves.

The sun had been awake several hours before Vela helped secure the ship to the dock for repairs. Muhif had given the sailors the week off and overall, everyone aboard acted happy.

At least until the ship docked.

From her spot by the deck railing, Vela watched a man dressed as a king's messenger waiting impatiently on the dock. She didn't pay much attention until he hurried up the gangway. The yellow crown embroidered onto his clothes made it easy to tell he came with the king's business.

The sailors stopped their work to watch when the messenger approached Muhif and handed him a paper which the sea captain scanned quickly. "Now?" he shouted in the messenger's face.

Vela clutched the railing. She had never seen Muhif so angry.

The startled messenger fell backward onto the deck. Then he rose and brushed himself off. "You can be most assured that she will go to the most experienced team," he replied stiffly.

"But she's only eighteen," Muhif protested.

"She started her training at the usual time," the messenger countered. He rubbed briskly at a blot that stained his otherwise spotless tunic.

Muhif sighed and nodded.

Vela was dying to know what they were talking about, but she dared not ask the messenger. Nor could she ask Muhif, for that matter, considering how her master had responded. She, like everyone aboard, knew Muhif would make an announcement in his own time.

So the sailors went back to work unloading.

The sea captain motioned Vela over to his side and handed her the paper. "You're being transferred to another team," he said sullenly. "I received a notice last year saying that you might be transferred due to the trouble Mevol was stirring up. But when nothing happened for a while, I thought you would be fine."

Vela's heart leapt high then flew into a wild beat as the prospect of leaving the sea hit her. How could her teacher have kept this information from her? "Do I have to go?"

Muhif nodded.

"Will I stay on the sea?"

He shook his head. "No, you won't."

"I'll get my things," she managed to mumble and left the over deck. Cook stopped her inside the hatch and asked what was wrong. "I'm getting transferred."

Cook gasped and shook his head. "No!"

Holding back tears, Vela pushed past him and ducked into her quarters. She stuffed her clothes in a bag and headed out to see her friend Daryla. Her feet pounded across the deck, down the gangplank, and over the wooden pier as she wiped a hand across her tear-filled eyes.

"Vela, what happened?" Daryla questioned as soon as she stepped out of her house.

I probably have tear stains all over my face, Vela thought. "I'm getting transferred so we won't see each other much anymore. It's a Watchman thing, but let's just make this last week happy, please."

Daryla nodded. "We can go fishing off the dock."

Vela was content with that.

A few nights later, she joined Muhif and his sailors at the tavern. None of them drank, but it was the only place to find good food. Having lost her appetite a while ago, Vela picked at her soup and bread.

Instead of joining the conversation, she surveyed the tavern. Most times when they docked, Vela stayed on board and ate with Cook. Those were her master's orders, but Muhif had decided to let her join the crew this last time.

This particular tavern was small for a port the size of Sail Village. However, considering there were several other taverns, it was understandable. The main floor consisted of a dining room with tables, benches, and stools scattered around.

A door in the back led to what Vela guessed was the kitchen. The narrow stairway situated next to the kitchen door most likely guided travelers to beds they could rent for a few evenings.

One thing caught Vela's interest the most this evening. A black cloaked man sitting in a corner of the tavern. When she glanced over at him, she caught him staring at her.

How unsettling.

"Ye stole me coin pouch!" someone shouted just then.

A man stood and towered over another man at a nearby table. His glare looked dark and slightly fuzzy. His companion shrank back. It was obvious the shouter had a reputation for getting angry after he had too much to drink.

"No, no, I didn't! 'T'was that man over there." He pointed to the black-cloaked man in the corner, the one who had made Vela's curiosity climb so high.

Both men were drunk. Vela clearly saw the coin pouch hanging from the accuser's belt.

Hidden away in the corner, the cloaked figure had been relaxing in his chair. Now, he grew alert as the angry man turned on him. Seething with anger, the man stalked over and slammed his hand down on the table.

Calmly, the cloaked man looked up. "Can I help you?"

"Give me pouch back or I'll pound ye true to the floor," he slurred, clearly the result of the mead he'd overindulged on.

"Sir, your pouch is on your belt. I didn't take it," the mysterious stranger replied. He took a drink from his cup as if he was falsely accused every day.

"I'll teach you to steal from me!" the accuser roared. He jerked the man to his feet by his shirt and threw a punch at him. The cloaked man ducked under the blow, grabbed his arm, and twisted it behind his back. He guided the man's hand until he could feel the pouch still on his belt.

"Your bag was there all along. I suggest you stay out of the tavern unless you want to spend a night in jail," he warned.

Then he released the man, dropped a few coins on the table, and headed toward the door. Stopping for a moment, the stranger glanced around. He met Vela's gaze for a moment before disappearing out the door.

The next morning, Vela woke in her hammock like always. Today she would leave all that she knew. Sadly, she packed her belongings in a small bag and made sure her white-and-blue uniform was spotless. She went up on deck, where Muhif, not a man of many words, stood. He had already talked to her last night, knowing that she would want to get an early start in the morning. Muhif shook her hand solemnly.

Vela walked down the gangplank, crossed the pier, and turned onto the road. She waved at her shipmates until the road curved and the trees blocked her view. It was a long walk to the Command Center, and her journey had only just begun.

Chapter Two

Wurren shifted his sword into a more comfortable position as he guided his horse to the dock. A Watchman ship bobbed alongside the pier and a muscular man was directing some sailors in their work. Narrowing his eyes at the man, Wurren stopped his horse a few paces away and waited. Finally, the big man turned around and glared at him.

"What do you want?" the man demanded.

He probably thinks I'm a land-lubber Watchman. The thought flicked across Wurren's mind. A slight smirk creased his face.

"I was sent by Commodore Louris to escort an apprentice to the Command Center," he announced, dismounting smoothly.

The big seaman responded in an icy voice, "She already left."

"Which way did she take?" Wurren asked.

"The road north out of town."

The young Watchman thanked him, mounted, and set his horse to a trot.

It wasn't long before he heard a cry coming from the road ahead. It sounded like a woman's cry of surprise.

Pressing his heels gently into his horse's sides, they took off at a canter around a bend and slid to a stop. A creak of leather accompanied the rustling of fabric as Wurren dismounted and drew his sword at the same time.

Three men had waylaid a girl. He had no doubt it was the apprentice, Vela. It was equally obvious that the ruffians were intent on getting whatever bit of money she might be carrying.

"Worthless thieves," he muttered. They wandered the countryside terrorizing travelers. The young man ran toward them, holding his sword in his right hand.

The thieves fled carrying one of their party. He appeared unconscious, thanks to Vela.

"Thank you," she exclaimed. "They took me by surprise."

"Don't thank me. I was just close enough to hear the fight." Wurren studied Vela for a minute. He shoved back his unruly black hair that had become even more disheveled by his fast ride.

Pushing back his cloak, he returned his sword to the scabbard that hung from a belt around his brown-leather jerkin. "You look like a Watchman from the Sails," he commented, indicating the chain around her neck that held the small anchor.

"Vela, apprentice of Muhif of the Sails," she replied. Then she gasped and looked closer at his face. "You're the man from the tavern!"

"My name is Wurren." He gave Vela a half bow. "Commodore Louris sent me to escort you to the Command Center. And, aye, that was me in the tavern."

Vela looked at the young man through suspicious eyes as she remembered the event a few days ago. "Why did you keep staring at me in the tavern?" She didn't want to admit that his stare had scared her half to death.

"I noticed that you were with Muhif's crew and thought that you might be the apprentice I was sent to escort."

"Well, thank you again, but I can manage by myself."

Wurren raised an eyebrow. "Even after what just happened here?" His green eyes lost their glint of mirth. "Roadside robberies are normally worse than what you experienced."

"I guess I *could* use a little help," Vela admitted sheepishly. "I don't really know where I'm going."

Smiling, Wurren motioned toward his horse. "Let's go then. We've got a long way to go, but I'm sure Twilight will have no problem carrying the both of us."

"I don't know how to ride."

"Hmm." He looked at Vela thoughtfully. "Well, that's a problem. But we can work on it while we travel."

Swinging up onto Twilight, he held out his hand to Vela who accepted it a little hesitantly. "Set your right foot in here," he instructed. "Aye, that's called a stirrup. Now swing yourself up and the other leg goes over the back of the horse. There. You can hold onto my shoulders if you like so you don't fall off."

After a minute of gentle trotting, he asked, "How long have you been on a ship?"

Feeling like she could trust him, Vela told her story. "My father was a successful merchant. He took my mother and me with him starting before I was ten. When I was sixteen, my love for the sea hadn't wavered, so I joined the Sails as an apprentice."

After another moment of silence, Vela asked a question of her own. "Have you seen the Phoenix team?"

"I heard they were phantoms," Wurren answered slowly.

"I didn't think they were real either. At sea, the older sailors told me they were phantoms made to scare the Mevolen away. And that they would kill anyone rather than look at them, including other Watchmen."

Wurren laughed. "No, we—ah, they're not phantoms."

Vela smiled inwardly. She was sure that they made a strange pair to any onlooker. Her companion talked little of the team he was from and she tried not to speak of the Sails. It still hurt too much. They met in the middle instead and talked about where they were from and the like. It turned out that Wurren hailed from near the Command Center, so he clearly knew his way around well.

It was dark before Wurren and Vela stopped at a small stone house with an even tinier lean-to behind it. He took care of Twilight then led Vela inside. The candle Wurren lit flickered and threatened to go out but then steadied after a moment and grew brighter. Through the dim light, Vela saw one pallet on the floor, along with a rough wooden table and two chairs. The rest of the house was empty.

Wurren set the candle on the table and pulled bread and dried meat from one of the saddlebags he had brought inside with him. "This was built for Watchmen that are traveling to a different place," he explained. "It's small but comfortable."

"When will we get to the Command Center?" Vela asked, studying the dimly lit room.

"Day after tomorrow, late afternoon." Wurren handed her some dried meat and two slices of bread.

Vela's legs and thighs ached. So did her back. "I hurt all over," she groaned.

Wurren nodded. "You're not accustomed to being on a horse for most of the day." He motioned for her to take the pallet.

"Where are you going to sleep?" Vela scanned the room again to see if she had missed another pallet or bed, but there was none.

"I'll sleep on the floor. You might want to learn that you shouldn't be picky about your bed here on land," he remarked.

Vela didn't argue. She was too tired.

Tired or not, Wurren woke her up bright and early the next morning. A quick meal and they were off again. The two passed through several small villages and one large town. They were all bustling with activity. Everyone looked warily at the Watchmen as they rode by.

Watchmen were clearly still mysterious and sort of creepy to the villagers. Wurren explained that just recently did the Asterians actually figure out that the Watchmen were real and not just tall tales.

Wurren's prediction came true about their arrival time. In the late afternoon of the third day, Vela found herself standing in front of a tall stone tower, trying to summon the courage to open the door. Finally, she opened the door and found herself in a big meeting room. The walls were adorned with tapestries of the history of Asteri, the Breaking, the forming of the League of Watchmen, and others. A long table spread out in the middle of the room, surrounded by tall, straight-backed chairs.

The Breaking sure was an interesting part of history. She thought. *It's hard to believe Asteri was once a part of Mevol.*

An older woman, who looked like a secretary, approached. "May I help you?" she asked.

"I'm an apprentice here to see the commodore about a transfer," Vela murmured.

"Ah, aye. Come with me."

Vela was soon led up a flight of steep stairs and into a short hallway, where the secretary knocked on the first door.

"Come in," came the muffled answer.

Vela entered and glanced around the room.

Commodore Louris looked younger than Vela had supposed he was. Light brown hair was cut close to his head, and brown eyes sized her up as soon as she'd entered. He sat at a desk that was very organized, with only a few messages scattered on the top.

"Ah, Vela of the Sails. Come, sit down." He stood up and pulled out a chair for her.

"Thank you, sir." She timidly sat on the edge of her seat.

"I heard from my messenger that Muhif didn't like my decision."

"He wasn't too happy, sir," Vela answered carefully, trying not to get Muhif in trouble.

"Please drop the sir. It makes me feel old."

A smile tugged at the corners of Vela's mouth. It was impossible not to like the commodore, unless of course, you were Mevolen. He made her feel at home immediately with his kind smile and easy-going actions.

There was a smart rap on the door and Wurren came in, closing the door behind him. "You wanted to see me, sir?"

"Wurren, captain of the Phoenix team, nice to see you again." Commodore Louris stood and greeted Wurren warmly.

Vela felt a flame of embarrassment flick up her cheeks. "C-Captain," she stuttered. "Phoenix?"

"I'm sorry I didn't tell you. I wanted you to feel at ease." A look of apology flashed across Wurren's face. He stood with his leather gloves held in one hand.

"Is everything all right?" Louris seemed concerned.

"Aye, Father, just legends," Wurren assured him.

Vela felt like a wildfire had overtaken her face. *Wurren is the commodore's son.* Why hadn't she been more careful about what she'd said earlier?

"Oh, legends." The Commodore waved a careless hand. "They are everywhere, even on the seas. Wurren, when are you due back at your base?"

"Two days from tomorrow."

"I guess you could take Vela to her team then too." He turned away.

Vela frowned. Was he hiding a smile behind his hand? What was going on?

"Excuse me, sir?" Wurren sounded as confused as Vela felt.

"She's your apprentice now." Louris clearly enjoyed being blunt.

Vela's mouth dropped open. "W-what?"

"Please, not right now, sir," Wurren pleaded. "Not after what happened. I don't think the team could handle it."

"You'll probably need all the help you can get here soon. Anyway, I already promised Muhif that she would be sent to the best team and your team is the best." The commodore's voice left no room for excuses though it was tinged with a hint of sorrow.

The young captain sighed and nodded. "Aye, sir."

Louris extended his hand to Vela and waited.

After a moment of confusion, Vela realized what he wanted. Slowly, she reached around her neck, drew the Sail pendant up over her head, and placed it in his hands.

In his own turn, Wurren reached out and took another pendant that the Commodore handed him and gave it to Vela. She fingered the silver Phoenix for a moment before, with a long sigh, she slipped it over her head to replace her old one.

"You two can stay here tonight and continue on tomorrow." Louris turned back to the papers on his desk, signaling that the conversation was over.

They stepped out of the room, Wurren closing the door softly behind him. A strange look was stamped on his features, a mixture of anger, confusion, and exasperation.

"Are you angry with me?" Vela desperately hoped for the opposite.

"No, just bad memories." Wurren shook his head and walked down the hall. "You can stay in there." He motioned to a door then opened his own across the hallway. From the glance she caught of it, his room seemed to be simple, but a few small figures were scattered on the table.

Pushing open her own door, Vela found a room similar to Wurren's. It looked just like the stone house they had stayed in, except a hot supper was waiting on the table in this room. Grateful for the food, she collapsed into the chair and quickly devoured the hot stew before falling into her bed.

"What is going on?" she mused aloud. "First, I get taken from my group to be transferred to another one. Next, I might have just insulted the captain of my new team. Not the best way to start out."

Lying in bed, Vela's eyelids started to droop. She could already feel her muscles protesting to the new way of traveling through her sleepiness.

But in a moment, not even that disturbed her rest.

Chapter Three

Wurren was fingering a few small children's toys that he had left here at his last visit. They were carved wood, some knights and horses, but they brought back painful memories. His mind was so far away that he jumped when a knock sounded at the door.

Shaking his head at being so nervous, he called, "Come in." He turned around as Commodore Louris entered. "Father? Is there something I can do for you?"

"Aye. We've begun to get these letters from somewhere in Mevol. They tell us about the different city strengths, outposts, ships, and even when and where raids might happen. And that in a few years, they're planning a full-scale attack."

"They're *what?*"

Wurren could hardly believe his ears. The Mevolen war lords had tried some crazy things in the past, but they were normally too busy disagreeing and fighting each other to team up against Asteri.

Louris handed him papers dating back to a year and a half ago.

Wurren skimmed them and looked up. "Are they true, sir?"

"We have stopped some of them. But I'm worried that some time there might be an ambush for us instead of a raid."

"Are the letters signed?" Wurren scanned the documents for a signature.

"Aye. There was an 'M' on the letters until a year ago, when another sign appeared that I thought might interest you." The commodore pointed to a symbol in the bottom right-hand corner of the page. "I've been trying to let you look at these, but it's taken a while."

"A Phoenix." The young captain let out a breath as he caught sight of the object of interest.

When Vela woke up and found she wasn't in her hammock, she jumped out of bed only to fall back onto the blankets. "Ouch!" She gasped when a white-hot flare of pain flitted through her sore muscles. With a sigh, she remembered her long horseback ride yesterday.

Vela saw a hot bowl of mush on the table, which was soon gone. With her stomach full, she studied her new pendant then left it to dangle on the outside of her white tunic.

A knock at the door caught Vela's attention, and Wurren's muffled voice came through. "We're leaving now."

"Coming." Grabbing her bag, Vela straightened her shoulders, opened the door, and walked past Wurren, ready to face another painful ride.

He mounted Twilight and held out his hand to her.

Vela hesitated. *I'd rather walk instead of ride, but I guess that doesn't work.* Accepting his hand, she swung up and sat behind him.

When the rains came, Wurren handed Vela a spare cloak and kept riding. The rain grew harder. It pounded the ground all around them. Wurren guided Twilight under a large tree that gave them a little shelter from the rain. They ate, and Wurren said he would keep watch for a little while.

While his charge slept peacefully, the young captain's eyes took on a faraway look, and figures began to dance before them. Times Wurren didn't want to remember...

A dead horse lying in a clearing with blood covering the ground; Watchmen shouting someone's name; a thin, silver chain covered in blood. Then the image of the person floated through Wurren's mind. He had been very close to the last apprentice he had been training when it had happened.

Shaking his head to clear his mind of the image, Wurren's eyes probed the darkness for any sign of someone nearby. Nothing appeared to endanger the two travelers, though. So at last, eyes drooping, he fell into a fitful sleep.

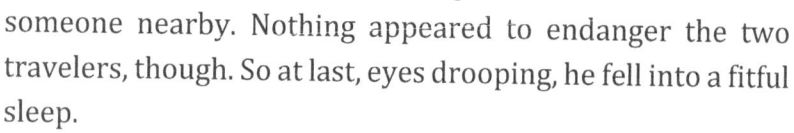

The next day passed the same. A blur of traveling through the rain, few words exchanged. The only difference was that they slept in another stone house. Apparently, Vela had gotten used to the soreness of riding. She didn't mention it again.

After a while, the rain worked its way through the waxed cloaks the Watchmen wore, chilling Wurren to the bone.

Vela shivered. She too must be chilled. For a moment, Wurren felt a sliver of compassion for the young woman, but it quickly faded. *She must learn hardships one way or another.*

This soaking, chilly weather kept up for the next several days until it changed to a grey, overcast sky. It seemed to drape a foul mood over everything and darken any sunshine that managed to creep through. The roads they traveled turned muddy and the creeks ran deep, but at least the rain had stopped. Wurren felt less tired and sat up straighter when they neared a clearing and Vela's new home.

"Welcome to your new home." He swept an arm across the clearing that showed a large, two-story wooden cabin with an accompanying stable. A wood fence surrounded a field behind the cabin, but it seemed strangely unoccupied.

The homely cabin was constructed of rough, heavy logs. *The windows and door make the front of the cabin look like a gaping mouth.* The thought ran across Wurren's mind, not for the first time.

He reined in Twilight, a nagging feeling in his brain. "Something's not right."

The horse nickered and turned his head to the right of the clearing. "You might want to hold on and keep low," Wurren warned and urged Twilight forward.

It took only a few strides for the grey horse to launch into a full gallop. When he did, Wurren heard Vela's small gasp of surprise. Trees and bushes whizzed past as he leaned over Twilight's neck. A thick stand of trees flew up in front of them. Just as they passed it, a horn blared. Twilight turned sharply in that direction and brought his riders to a rocky field that gradually slanted upwards.

Three figures cloaked similarly to himself were in a fight for their lives. A child frozen in fear seemed to be the objective of the twenty warriors who now surrounded them. Swords flashed dully. The clang of steel on steel echoed through the trees.

"Get off and stay here," Wurren ordered when they were still a good distance from the skirmish. He handed her a long knife. "I hope you don't have to use this."

Drawing his sword, Wurren yelled and charged Twilight at the circle of flashing blades.

The enemies, whom Vela identified as Mevolen warriors, looked surprised by an attack from behind. She gazed in wonder while Wurren slashed his way towards his friends. She had often seen skirmishes on the sea, but this was nothing like what she had seen.

With powerful build and bulging muscles, the Mevolen attackers surrounded the three cloaked figures. The enemy warriors wore thick metal armor that seemed to somewhat restrict their movements with the heavy battle axes they bore.

Vela knew from her studies that only the higher-ranking soldiers and lords were granted the privilege to use swords and even those were curved *talwars*. This meant that these men were the lower-ranking soldiers. Mevolens relied on brute strength and numbers to overcome their enemies.

Sometimes, that tactic worked.

Vela's attention was averted when she saw a warrior step out from behind a tree one sword-length away to her left. He raised his ax and sliced at her head. Vela ducked the blow, and the ax stuck in the tree trunk right where her head had been a second ago. She jumped towards the man, sank her dirk into a joint between the shoulder armor, and pulled it out.

The man roared in pain and drew his own long knife. Not expecting this, Vela barely dodged the blade before slicing the man's wrist. Blood spurted from the wound and distracted the warrior long enough so she could trip him and knife him again. He muttered a few words in his native language.

Vela's ears burned at being called a "pesky little brat." But the man was gone already, so there was nothing she could do.

Looking up, Vela found the Mevolen warriors retreating towards a summit in the mountains. By their dress, she assumed that these people were part of her new team. They had won against impossible odds. *They must be very experienced to fight off so many warriors this quickly,* she thought.

A little way away, the Watchmen were leaning on their swords laughing. Laughing! *How can they be so happy when they could have been killed?* Through the slightly cool air, their conversation drifted down to her. She listened to learn what type of people she was going to meet.

"You came just at the right time, Wurren." One of the men clapped him on the back while sheathing his sword. "Did you see that man's face, Gliese?"

"Aye, he turned as white as mist."

Another of the group, a young lady asked, "What did Louris want you to do *this* time?" She whistled and several horses trotted up, with a villager running not far behind.

"Thank you for saving my son," he cried, scooping a small boy up in his arms. The one called Gliese took him aside and told him something before the villager left.

"So?" the woman asked.

"You *are* impatient, aren't you, Ankaa?" Wurren gave a brief smile and started walking back toward Twilight. The others trailed him. "He wanted me to escort an apprentice to the Command Center. She was being reassigned."

The Watchmen and their horses picked their way in her direction. Vela ducked back to where Wurren had left her.

A look of surprise flashed across Wurren's face he glanced over Vela's shoulder at the dead man. She handed him the carefully cleaned dagger and said, "I have had some training, you know."

She turned and studied the rest of the team. The smiles had disappeared from their faces as soon as they saw Vela. It was obvious they disliked the idea of having another person on their team.

"You mean, reassigned *here*." Ankaa's voice lost its spark.

Vela felt a chill run down her spine at the woman's unwelcoming words.

Chapter Four

"Vela, this is Ankaa, Kappa, and Gliese. Team, this is Vela from the Sails. She will be the new member of our team." Wurren appeared to be slightly discomforted as he introduced her.

The rest of the group clasped forearms with her in the traditional greeting, but Vela could tell they were hesitant in accepting her. It felt like a cold wall had come up between them, and she didn't mean for it to be that way. *What have I ever done to them?*

She mounted up behind Wurren who matched Twilight's gait with that of the other horses. Silence reigned over the party until they reached the cabin.

Vela could now get a closer look at the cabin and found that the walls of the cabin and stable had been smeared with a yellowish mix. It looked like the fireproof mix they used at sea. Several windows on the second floor indicated more rooms. The cabin looked big enough to hold them all comfortably.

Each Watchman took care of his or her own horse in the stable before going through a door that looked like it led to the cabin. None spoke a word to Vela or to their captain.

"Don't worry about them," Wurren assured her. "It's been a while since we had a new person around here."

The young captain's assurance didn't change the fact that Vela knew she was rejected. Trying to find a reason to be more cheerful, she switched the topic. "I recognized Kappa, I think. I met you two at the Watchman Challenge a year ago, right? You got shot with that blunted arrow. I was curious when the commodore said you guys were only visitors." Vela thought back to the annual event that every Watchman attended.

The challenge was filled with competitions and games that kept the Watchmen sharp and taught them to work together. It was held in different locations every year so that the Watchmen could get the experience of other terrains.

"Aye, that was us," Wurren replied. "Why don't we go inside?" He motioned for Vela to enter the doorway through which the others had gone, and she nodded before taking one more glance around.

Now, she could see inside the stable. Stalls lined a wall, with the horses' tack hanging on the wall opposite their stalls. Straw littered the floor and two doors at the end of the stable looked to open to storage and training rooms. A hint of dust in the air made Vela sneeze.

Wurren raised an eyebrow before grabbing his bags and entering the door connecting the stable to the cabin. He led her through the armory, which seemed to be well stocked, and into a main room that held a table and six chairs. More comfy chairs sat closer to the fireplace at the other end, probably for lounging in the evenings.

"Ankaa, could you please show Vela where she will stay?" Wurren asked when they all gathered inside.

"Sure thing," she replied sullenly.

With her cloak removed, Vela could see that Ankaa was a tall, blonde-haired young woman in her younger twenties. Serious blue eyes studied Vela as they climbed the stairs to the second floor.

Vela glanced around the room she was shown. They looked the same from what she could tell through the open doorways. Two beds in each room, a small fireplace, and a chest stood at the foot of each bed for clothes.

"You'll stay here with me." Ankaa fidgeted in the doorway then said, "Sorry for the cold reception. Can we be friends?"

Vela felt a smile spread across her face. "I would love to."

"What sea captain were you with?" Ankaa asked, returning the smile.

"Captain Muhif."

"Muhif? I've heard stories of him. Well, mostly about his strength. He is the one I'm thinking of, right?" The two girls sat on their beds across from each other.

"Aye," Vela replied. "I saw him knock two sailors' heads together because they were fighting. But my favorite person on board was Cook. He was kind to me. Where did you grow up?"

"A day's walk away from the Command Center. My father was the tailor of our village."

Downstairs, the men were having a somewhat heated discussion about their new apprentice.

"Why is she here?" Gliese demanded.

"I don't know." Wurren stacked the leftover supplies in a cupboard.

"The commodore thought we needed help?" Kappa asked. He entered the room and began to bandage Gliese's arm. "Ankaa has already made friends with her. I saw them talking upstairs." His tone showed that he was displeased with this.

Wurren studied his friends. Gliese was half a year older than Wurren with light-brown hair and twinkling brown eyes. Kappa, on the other hand, was sterner and a whole year older than his captain.

"Apparently so." The captain shrugged. "There's nothing we can do about the assignment. I didn't find out about it till halfway through our journey. But she has improved since we first met."

Gliese raised his eyebrows, making him look serious for once in his life. "How so?"

"Well..." Wurren thought for a moment. "She didn't know how to ride at first."

The oldest Watchman, Kappa, rolled his eyes, but didn't comment.

"That changed fast," Wurren went on. "Don't expect her to know a lot. She says she's been on the seas for more than eight years."

Kappa started to make supper, flicking his dark-brown hair out of his eyes with a finger. "Yes, riding is a very good thing to know if you're on land. But didn't the commodore remember what happened to our last apprentice? We don't need another one."

"He said we needed all the help we could get," Wurren repeated tersely.

"I hope she can cook. It might be better than your cooking," Gliese teased Kappa, then ducked out of the room before Wurren could say anything.

The cook shook his head and muttered, "He needs to grow up." Kappa's blue eyes took the good-natured teasing in stride.

Supper turned out to be simple, with the hot soup Kappa made and delicious bread. The soup consisted of chunks of meat, herbs, potatoes, celery, and tomatoes. Ankaa used the bread to sop up the remaining liquid in her bowl so she wouldn't miss a drop of the mouthwatering meal.

During the meal, Wurren brought up a question he needed to ask. "Anything go wrong while I was away?" Ankaa, Gliese, and Kappa looked at each other then back at Wurren.

"What? Wrong? Oh no, nothing went wrong," Gliese stammered.

"No, nothing at all," Ankaa put in.

Vela looked up from her bowl of soup and grinned at the excuses the two Watchmen made.

"What happened, Kappa?" Wurren looked towards his lieutenant.

"Let's see." Kappa tilted his chair back and thought for a minute. "To start with, Gliese got the firewood wet, so when Ankaa started the kitchen fire for dinner yesterday, the whole room filled with smoke. Then I tripped over a string across my doorway when I came out to see about all the smoke." He grimaced. "But other than that, everything went fine."

"Gliese?" Wurren turned to the mischief maker.

The accused raised his hands in defense. "Sorry. Everything is always boring when you're gone."

"Not with you around." Ankaa elbowed him in the ribs, and he doubled over in exaggerated pain. "Are there any people aboard your ship that keep things as exciting as Gliese does?" She turned to Vela, who had kept silent during the meal.

Vela hesitated before answering. "The only exciting thing is trying to catch the sailors who exchange Cook's fresh water with salt water. There isn't much else to do on a ship that the rest of the crew doesn't see. The other thing is... if you turn the hourglass too soon in the captain's quarters. But the last person who did that got fired and thrown into the bay."

"Haven't heard of the water prank before," Gliese said thoughtfully. "Maybe I should try it." Then his face fell. "But we don't have any salt water around here."

"If you ruin one more meal, Gliese, *you'll* miss a meal," Kappa threatened. Ankaa snickered.

"Was the attack on a village?"

Vela's soft question caught Wurren's attention, and the attention of the others. The banter stopped. Four sets of eyes glanced at one another before settling on Vela.

After a minute of intense silence, Wurren thought he would have to tell her, but Ankaa spoke up. "Aye. The Mevolens raid the villages near the borders and take young children to work as slaves. This recent raid was on a farm a few miles from here. Most of the children that go missing during the raids are from five to sixteen years old. Sometimes adults go missing too."

Pain flashed across Vela's face before she nodded and pushed away from the table. Ascending the stairs with rapid footsteps, she was out of sight in seconds.

"Should I have told her about that?" Ankaa asked.

"She would have to hear it sooner or later," Gliese pointed out.

Ankaa rose from her chair to follow her new friend, but Wurren held up his hand. "Give her a little time by herself. Whatever she's dealing with, we can help her after."

Ankaa nodded and cleared the dishes from the table.

"Any casualties from the raid?" asked Wurren.

"We caught it in time. The only worry was Gliese's arm, but even that was minor," Kappa reported confidently.

"Good." Wurren nodded. A few minutes later, he spotted Ankaa making her way towards the stairs.

Chapter Five

In her room, a terrible scene played out in Vela's mind's eye. A merchant ship trapped on two sides by Mevolen warships. Sailors lay strewn across the deck either dead, wounded, or fighting for their lives.

Screams came from inside the cabin, and four warriors appeared. One carried a young girl about ten years old swung over his shoulder like a sack of flour. Two other men dragged a young Vela across the deck and towards their ships.

A woman ran out of the cabin after them. She attacked one of the men's backs with a small dagger. Another raider wearing a bucket helmet over his face ran his sword through the woman.

The captain of the merchant ship saw his wife fall and yelled. Fighting violently, he engaged her murderer with his sword. Their weapons clashed. The two were evenly matched until the captain's foot caught on a barrel and he fell backward. Vela screamed as the blade plunged into her father's heart.

"Captain!" one of the pirates called. "Two Watchmen ships are approaching."

The captain motioned the man with the younger girl away. "Take that one on the other ship and escape." He pointed at the other pirates. "You. Finish with the sailors and get my ship underway."

The Mevolen captain grabbed Vela's arm and pulled her off her father's ship and onto his own, making sure her hands were securely tied.

But it was too late for him. A Watchman ship pulled alongside as the captain thrust Vela into a dark room and closed the door. All she could hear were scuffles and yelling from outside. Then the noises stopped and she heard the sound of people running everywhere. Smoke began to seep in under the door. It was getting harder to breathe.

Muhif found her there. Vela begged him to take her as his apprentice to stop these horrible kidnapping raids. He assented. She later learned that the other ship with the younger girl on board had not been overtaken.

A knock on the door shook Vela from her nightmare. She jumped, startled.

Ankaa peeked in and frowned her concern. "Did I say something wrong?"

Vela shook her head and quickly wiped the back of her hand across her eyes. "No. I just needed time by myself."

"What's the matter?" Ankaa slipped in and sat on a nearby chest.

"I should probably tell you how I became a Watchmen." Vela took a deep breath and slowly let it out to calm her heart that pounded in her chest.

"You don't have to tell me if you don't want to," Ankaa assured her.

"No, there is a time to mourn and a time to rejoice, so I will share this with you. But you can tell no one. When you were talking about the poor children getting taken, it reminded me of how I was almost taken." Vela revealed her story to Ankaa. Telling how she was orphaned, her younger sister stolen, and how she started her next few years as an apprentice.

Vela had told nobody her story until now. Not even Muhif knew the whole story, even though he had rescued her.

Ankaa sat in stunned silence. Then she said, "I'm so sorry."

"There's nothing you—or anyone—can do about it." Vela turned towards the window and didn't speak. The only sound she heard was the door closing softly behind Ankaa.

Vela stared out the window into the sunset. She wondered for the first time in years if her little sister was looking at that same sunset.

Wurren was waiting out in hallway when Ankaa came out of the room. "Is she all right?"

"Aye. I promised not to repeat the story. But I can tell you that she's an orphan and her parents were murdered right before her eyes." She clattered down the steps.

Wurren nodded thoughtfully then turned and headed for his room.

It took some time to fall asleep, but the next morning he was happy to wake up in his own bed. Glancing out the window at the torrent of rain falling, he groaned. *I was hoping to have a nice long ride today.*

He threw off his bed covers, rose to his feet, and found a long-sleeved, dark-green tunic and brown pants in his chest. Slipping on a sleeveless brown, leather jerkin over the tunic, he crossed the room and pulled his cloak off the rack, where it had been hung to dry next to the fire. Checking to make sure his knives were on his belt, Wurren made his way downstairs.

Gliese was already in the kitchen heating up water for coffee and tea. When the captain entered the room and mumbled a "good morning," Gliese acknowledged his presence with a quick nod. Running a hand through his hair, Wurren closed his eyes and sniffed the delicious smell of raspberry leaf tea. *My favorite!*

"Good morning, Wurren," Gliese called cheerfully after the water was heated up. "Glad to be back yet?"

"Aye, after sleeping in my own bed." Wurren pulled half a dozen biscuits from a bin on a shelf and put them in a bowl.

Gliese turned back to stirring a large pot of oatmeal hanging over the fire. Using a wooden spoon, he scooped up some oatmeal and tasted it to make sure it was cooked all the way through.

"Morning." Ankaa yawned as she stumbled, still half asleep, into the kitchen.

"Are you tired, Ankaa?" Wurren raised his eyebrows in mock surprise.

She glared at him. "You do not know how many shifts we had to take while you were gone."

"Too many for my liking," Gliese complained.

"Does Kappa work you too hard? My sympathies." Wurren hid the smile that threatened to break out on his face.

Kappa slid into the kitchen as he always did, without a sound. "I heard everything you said. I'm hurt."

"Kappa, you know you're not supposed to snoop on other people's conversations," Ankaa scolded.

"I wasn't snooping, I was spying. There's a difference."

Wurren smiled.

Ankaa looked at Gliese for help. "Is there a difference?" He shook his head and Ankaa grinned triumphantly at Kappa.

He shrugged. "Well, there is to me."

Still stirring breakfast, Gliese swung the big pot off the fire and called, "Breakfast is ready."

There was a shuffling noise and Wurren turned to see Vela come in. Her cheeks held a tint of pink indicating that she had been outside for some time.

"What have you been doing?" Ankaa filled her bowl with oatmeal, milk, and berries and sat down at the table.

"Admiring the horses," Vela said. "They are all beautiful. I couldn't see many of them on the sea."

From behind Vela's back, Kappa roll his eyes in annoyance before dishing up his breakfast.

After the delicious meal, Wurren sent the two girls upstairs. "Help Vela get outfitted properly for the terrain," he instructed Ankaa. When the girls had disappeared up the stairs, he looked at Kappa. "As much as we all don't want her here, she is going to stay. You might as well get used to it and not mock her. Vela can't help how she's grown up."

Kappa shook his head. "But Wurren, riding? She seriously didn't know how to ride?"

"Commodore Louris must have seen something in her at the past two Challenges she's attended. We must figure out what that is and help her advance in that area. It's our duty. No excuses." Wurren's tone meant business.

Kappa nodded, and his mouth sealed shut.

Dismissing Kappa to go scout, Wurren helped Gliese pick up the kitchen then asked him to find the girls.

When Vela descended the stairs, she seemed to be properly outfitted in something similar to his own clothes, except for a longer tunic. He addressed them quickly and thoroughly. "Ankaa, at midday, please ride to relieve Kappa on duty at the abandoned cabin."

Ankaa shivered. "Oh. You know how much I don't like that place."

"What cabin?" Vela asked.

"The Phoenix group was weaker at the beginning of the Breaking Age. A few attacks and they were wiped out. The old cabin they lived in lies half a mile west." Wurren pointed in the direction of the rising sun. "It was a few years ago that Commodore Louris decided to turn us into a legend. He picked the best young Watchmen and sent them to this new base location. The villagers reported seeing strange people in the mountainside forests. Our predecessors had to make chaos in a few Mevolen villages to spread the legends into Mevol. Disappearing and appearing at will along with the fact that they were never caught anchored the myths into these mountains. They scared the Mevolen away with the idea that they're phantoms."

Vela's face turned red.

Wurren smiled. "As you can see, we are absolutely not *phantoms*."

"Is something the matter, Vela? Your face turned ten shades of red."

Vela's cheeks turned a few shades darker. "At sea I heard legends about you. It was said that you Phantoms would kill anyone rather than look at them."

"Never heard of myself described that way before," Ankaa said after a minute of thought.

Wurren grinned. "I'll take you to find your weapons, Vela," he said, bringing the conversation to a close.

He led her to the armory and watched while Vela inspected their cache of weapons. Several recurve bows hung on the wall. Quivers of arrows and javelins stood in boxes at the back of the room. Extra swords rested on racks built into the wall, and an assortment of knives lay in a box next to the rack.

Wurren strung one of the recurves, handed Vela the bow, and asked how far she could pull it back. She looked unfamiliar with a recurve but Vela put the bow in her left hand and slowly pulled on the string until it rested against her cheek.

He nodded. "Good enough. We'll go outside to shoot once the rain stops."

She glanced outside at the pouring rain. "Uh, when will it stop?"

Wurren didn't glance up from the boxes he was rifling though. "Probably some time tonight or tomorrow." He came up with three knives of different sizes. "The smallest knife goes in your boot. You use this larger one for hand-to-hand combat." Wurren held up a middle-sized knife. "Sometimes if you must, you'll find yourself using this one, but it's mostly a throwing knife."

Vela studied each knife carefully before she slid the leather sheaths on her belt.

"Pick up the sword on the end of the rack," he ordered.

She did so. "It's rather lightweight," she remarked.

Wurren nodded and continued. "Here, we always carry our swords with us, in case an attack comes and we have to get to the villages quickly."

"Will we be able to practice today?"

Wurren smiled a little at the look of hopefulness on her face. "Aye. Thankfully, we made a room in the stable for sword fighting. But first, before we practice, there's someone I'd like you to meet."

Vela buckled the sword to her belt, and Wurren led her to the stables. Most of the horses were inside munching contentedly on the hay from the well-stocked cradles in their stalls. Gliese's mount was missing.

"You're going to need a horse to ride," Wurren said. "We have three that you can pick from." Wurren showed her a young brown and black stallion, a smaller black mare, and an older, spotted cream and black stallion.

Vela studied the horses for a minute before turning to him. "I'm no good judge of horses," she admitted. "What are they like?"

"If you want a seasoned, more obedient stallion, there's the black and cream one. The stallion is a little older. He sires the others, so he wouldn't be the best choice. The mare has a bad attitude and might be a good one, but only if you want a rough start. But the last one is a little impetuous."

Vela stroked each one. The older stallion stood rigid for a second then nipped her hand gently. The mare basked in the attention then went on munching hay. The younger stallion rubbed against her hands and looked straight into her eyes.

"I like this one." Vela moved her hand down to a place on his neck and scratched. The horse closed his eyes. His top lip folded up like he was making a silly face and his head bobbed up and down.

Wurren grinned at the comical sight and leaned against the wall. "He's yours then."

"Really? What's his name?"

"He doesn't have a name yet. That's your job. But for now, let's start with sword practice." He pushed away from the wall and led Vela to the training room.

Once inside, Wurren spun around. He drew his sword in one smooth motion that took less than a second.

Vela's sword rasped from the scabbard in a slow process until the point came clear.

A sigh escaped Wurren's mouth. *This is going to take longer than I thought.* He shook his head and showed her how to hold and pull out the sword the right way. She tried and accomplished it slightly faster than before, but it still needed work. *A lot of work.*

With the ease of an expert, Wurren showed her the many different guards and basic cuts. Vela was a fast learner. It looked like she knew the basics of sword fighting, but there was much she didn't know. Normally, an apprentice would learn the art of the sword during their apprenticeship and during their first few years as a full-fledged Watchman. But Wurren was sure it would take Vela a long time to learn everything.

Vela dragged herself inside after her miserable workout under Wurren. He was quite a taskmaster and swordsman. *I have a lot to learn,* she conceded, limping towards the stairs. She tried to ignore the young captain's amused look.

Just then, Vela heard hoof beats. She watched through the window and saw Gliese riding up sopping wet. He dismounted and led his horse into the stables they had just come from, saying, "Come on, Daga, let's get you inside."

A few minutes later, he threw open the door and stepped inside. "Looks like we're still phantoms after all. Those Mevolen warriors never made it back to their country."

Vela glanced from Gliese's dripping wet cloak to his triumphant face.

"Where did you go" demanded Wurren. "What do you mean?"

Vela paused at the bottom of the stairs and listened to what Gliese had to say for himself. She found it interesting to learn how they kept themselves a secret from nearly everyone in two whole countries.

"I went up to the pass and stayed on our side of the border," Gliese reported. "Even from our side you can see tracks of the warriors going back to the other side. Then they suddenly end in a pile of snow with no tracks leading away. I'm guessing they're buried under a snow fall."

Wurren looked thoughtful for a minute then said, "You went up there without telling anyone where you were going?"

Gliese nodded.

"What if the Mevolens had not been killed and were watching the border? They could have fallen upon you and either killed you or taken you away." Wurren paused and finished softly, "We don't need that again."

Reprimanded, Gliese quietly took to the stairs to change into dry clothes.

Vela left Wurren to himself and headed into the kitchen. Not long after she familiarized herself with the kitchen, she heard a horse ride into the stable and out from the rain. She had no trouble hearing Kappa talk to his horse while he rubbed him down. When he entered the kitchen to drop a cloth sack on the counter, he seemed surprised to find her there but gave her a cold nod before reporting to Wurren.

Vela sighed. Why was Kappa so quiet to her? He hadn't spoken a word to her since she came.

Vela managed to scrounge up something for dinner that tasted better than normal meals at sea. A good-sized slice of venison went on each plate, along with a dozen eggs she had scrambled. Her sea days with Cook had given Vela a few skills in the kitchen, but she wasn't a master.

Ankaa had taken her dinner with her and had not yet returned from patrol, so only Wurren, Kappa, Gliese, and herself. The meal was strangely silent.

After she finished wiping the dishes, Vela found Wurren. "Why has Kappa not said a single word to me?" she asked.

A flash of pain crossed Wurren's features. "He's not used to having an apprentice around," he explained. "We had an apprentice before you came. He went out on patrol, and we think a band of warriors surprised him. When we rode out to the area, we found his horse dead. However, we couldn't find-" Wurren looked too pained to say the apprentice's name. "Him. We searched the patrol area twice over, even crossed the border. We saw no sign. Nowhere."

"I'm so sorry." Her voice turned quiet.

Vela spent most of the afternoon in her room writing a letter to Muhif. Then she went to the dresser and pulled out a small, four-stringed instrument called a *kecil*. One of the older sailors on her parents' ship had taught her to play a number of ancient songs.

She played the first song, a haunting melody normally used when someone had died. But she liked the next song better, even though she made plenty of mistakes. She was sure nobody could hear her playing outside her room, and for that she was thankful.

A knock on the door startled Vela. She set her *kecil* in its waterproof case and stuffed it back in a drawer under her clothing. "Come in."

Gliese opened the door. "Supper time."

"Thank you." Vela made her way downstairs behind him. Ankaa had returned from patrol and smiled at Vela from her place at the table. Vela sat down beside her. As before, the meal carried on in silence, until Gliese cracked the tension by telling a joke that made everyone laugh.

After supper, Wurren asked Kappa if they could have some music. He nodded and tugged a wooden box from the shelf. Vela saw it held a violin. Setting it to his chin and drawing the bow across the strings, Kappa played a slow melody, one that was enough to put listeners to sleep.

Gliese sighed in exasperation, clearly hoping for something livelier.

Vela noticed the slightest smile in Kappa's face before he paused and tuned the violin. Then, a light song sprang from the instrument as if it was alive.

The bored young man sat up. He and Ankaa exchanged glances, then he jumped to his feet and twirled her into the middle of the room. Vela couldn't remember the last time she had seen a dance like that and was amazed at the intricacy.

Wurren started clapping in time to the music and Vela joined in. The two dancers collapsed back into their chairs once the song was over, gasping for breath.

"I haven't danced like that in a while." Ankaa gasped for air.

A smile covered Kappa's face, and he set his instrument down on his lap.

Wurren was laughing at Ankaa and Gliese, so Vela slipped away to get her *kecil*. When she returned, she saw that no one had noticed her absence. Nobody was looking at her now, either. She carefully placed her fingers on the *kecil* and plucked the strings. Out came a song she hadn't played since her parents had died and her sister was taken away.

The happy, carefree song turned the heads of the whole team. She kept playing even when Kappa joined in with his violin. The song was beautiful but slowed down until it finally stopped. Kappa caught Vela's eye and nodded almost like he approved of her playing.

"I didn't know you could play," Wurren said.

Vela nodded, a little shy. "I learned a couple of years ago. Good night."

Climbing the stairs, Vela's thoughts whirled. Maybe the land life of the Watchmen wasn't so bad. They joked with each other and pulled pranks.

Then her mind focused on that dance. A faint memory of learning the dance from her mother long ago stirred Vela's thoughts. All those memories opened the sorrow in her heart again.

Collapsing on her bed, she fell asleep.

Chapter Six

One of Vela's favorite subjects turned out to be archery. When the sun shone, Wurren or Ankaa took her outside and gave her pointers on aiming, though there was little she didn't already know. Vela only struggled with drawing the arrows from the quiver at her side. She had always pulled arrows from a quiver on her back, but she discovered that she could shoot faster with the quiver in a different place.

An adept archer already, Vela surprised the rest of the team with her accuracy and speed.

Riding was a different matter, however. Vela only knew how to ride behind someone and hang on. She knew nothing about riding alone. The first morning, Gliese showed her how to saddle her horse after Wurren asked him to. Vela stumbled with the heavy, awkward saddle, so Gliese helped her out.

Gliese motioned for her to mount and Vela's face turned red with embarrassment.

"I don't know how to mount," she mumbled.

Gliese sighed before patiently instructing her, and soon Vela had mastered the technique. Holding onto the pommel of the saddle, she placed her left foot in the stirrup. Then she gave a little jump, throwing her right leg across the horse's back and slipping her boot into the other stirrup.

But Vela's biggest challenge turned out to be finding the right name for her horse. A week passed, and her mount still had no name.

"Naming is so hard!" Vela complained to Ankaa.

"I know. It took me a while to find the right name too." Ankaa grinned as a sudden thought struck her. "You could call him Troublesome."

Vela laughed. Just yesterday, her horse had stopped suddenly, sending her flying over his head and onto the ground. "Maybe I will."

It took several weeks for Vela to get accustomed to the grueling training the Watchmen followed. Her sword skills improved at a steady rate and so did her horseback skills. But Kappa, Wurren, and Gliese still acted hesitant to accept her in missions.

After three months of training, Ankaa rode up at breakneck speed on her horse, Valiant, to where Vela fought Wurren in another training session, and she was desperately losing. "Captain!" Ankaa shouted. "Raiders are attacking the Southern Farm."

Wurren motioned Vela into the cabin. "Grab your bow and quiver. Keep your sword on and get Gliese while you're up there."

A tired Gliese answered Vela's pounding knock on his bedroom door. "What is it?"

"Raiders. Wurren wants you."

Grabbing her weapons, Vela ran back down into the stables pulling her cloak on as she ran. Ankaa had saddled Vela's horse for her. Gliese mounted last, but he looked wide awake now.

It was the first attack since Vela had arrived at the Phoenix base. Smoke rose above the treetops like grey, gangly fingers and screams split the air. Hoof beats shattered the still morning air as the Watchmen raced towards the farm.

At the top of a hill, Wurren assessed the situation. "I'm keeping Vela with me. Gliese, north side; Kappa, stay here; Ankaa, east side, and we'll take the west. Let none come out."

The Watchmen split up in different directions. Wurren pointed at where Gliese melted into the trees and let arrows fly. No one could tell where Kappa was. He had already disappeared.

"It's how we operate to keep our reputation as legends," he explained to Vela. "Strike from the shadows and avoid being seen."

Several Mevolen raiders started in Wurren's and Vela's direction. The raiders didn't see the threat but were instead trying to escape. One man held down a young woman across the front of his saddle. The prisoner screamed and kicked, doing her best to get free.

"I'll go after the man holding the girl. You get as many as possible," Wurren ordered.

Vela nodded, gripping her bow tightly till her knuckles turned white.

The raiders thundered towards the Watchmen's hiding place, oblivious to the hidden people.

"Now!"

When Wurren shot the raider holding the girl, she tumbled off the panicked horse and into a soft patch of grass. Vela held an arrow in her string hand while she shot the first shaft before loading the second one. The last raider screamed something about phantoms and Vela heard Wurren chuckle. Panicking, the remaining Mevolen tore off towards the border.

Wurren and Vela rode out of the bushes and Vela helped the young woman to her feet.

"Thank ya kindly fer savin' me." She looked up but then fell back to the ground gaping. "*Phantoms,*" she breathed, barely loud enough to hear.

Vela joined in the laughter. "We're not phantoms," she managed to say after she stopped laughing.

"We'd rather you not tell anyone, young miss," Wurren warned, but kindly. "It's how we keep the Mevolens away. We're human as much as you are."

The girl sighed in relief at Wurren's statement. "Ye's won't be hurtin' me?"

"Of course not. We just saved you," Wurren replied. "We can walk you back to the edge of the farm if you like."

"Aye, please."

Wurren turned to Vela. "Escort the young lady back to her farm. I will wait for the reports from the others."

"Aye, sir," Vela said. She walked her horse alongside the young woman, who still looked a little fearful. Clearly, she still couldn't believe the Phoenix team wasn't just a legend.

At the edge of the village, Vela stopped and took her arm. "Remember. Not a word. Got it?"

The farm girl nodded and ran in between the buildings.

Vela mounted and returned to Wurren, where she found the rest of the group waiting for her.

"Thank you, Vela." Wurren nodded then turned to his men. "Kappa and Gliese, follow the raiders and make sure they get back to their side of the border, where they belong." The two young men rode off with nods of confirmation.

The remaining Watchmen headed home and rode in silence. Vela watched the scenery go by as they made good time.

When they crested a hill, Ankaa squinted at their cabin a moment before saying, "Someone is there, Wurren."

"I noticed," the captain said, examining the distant horse. "I have a faint idea who it is."

Urging their horses forward, the Watchmen approached the cabin as someone came out to meet them. He wore a black cloak hanging from his shoulders. It fluttered in the breeze.

"Commodore Louris!" Vela exclaimed.

"I wonder why he came all the way out here," Ankaa commented. "Must be pretty important."

Wurren kept silent. If he knew why the commodore had dropped in unannounced, he wasn't sharing.

"Hello, Wurren, Phoenix team," Louris greeted the captain and the remaining team.

"Hello to you too, Father. Please give us a minute and we'll join you."

The commodore nodded to Wurren and went back inside.

After the team unsaddled their horses, they passed through the kitchen to the meeting room, leaving their cloaks and quivers on.

"What brings you here, Father?" asked Wurren. He sat down with the girls.

Instead of responding, Louris flipped a bundle of letters onto the table.

"I thought so." Wurren frowned, as if certain suspicions had just been confirmed. "What can we do for you?"

"I want you to take one or two of your team and go on a mission to find the sources of these letters."

"Is it necessary, Father? If the letters are true, use them to counter the Mevolens' attacks." Wurren gave the papers hardly more than a glance.

"In a normal case we would, but the letters have stopped arriving. If our informant has been caught, then the least we can do in return is to save them."

"Aye, sir." Wurren seemed in deep concentration. "I'll take Kappa and"—he set his jaw—"Vela."

Louris looked into Wurren's eyes. "Are you sure?"

Wurren took a deep breath. "I'm certain. It would be good training. We can disguise her as a boy if needed, but I hardly think that is necessary."

"Me?" asked Vela in disbelief.

"Aye, but you have to obey my every order." Her captain looked sternly at her.

"Aye, sir."

"The boys are back," Ankaa said. The creaking of leather from saddles and the small metallic clinks from their weapons gave them away.

"Someone is with them. That's too much noise from just two horses." Wurren rose from his chair and strung his bow. "Vela, take the upper window. Ankaa, armory. Nobody comes through that door unless they're friendly. Commodore, you might want to stay away from the windows. If they're after anyone, it would be you."

Louris looked on in silence while Ankaa and Wurren barred several doors and nocked their arrows. Vela darted up the stairs to peek out a second-story window. A small hole in the floor enabled her to talk to the others downstairs below.

"Umm, Captain? We have a problem," she said after a minute.

"What is it?"

Vela paused. How could she break this news? She took a deep breath. "There are about fifty Mevolen warriors outside. They've got Gliese and Kappa with them. Kappa has an arrow wound in his arm. I wonder how they found the cabin," she added as an afterthought.

"Great," she heard Ankaa mutter.

"Can you see the leader of the group, Vela?" Wurren shoved open one of the heavy wooden shutters then slammed it shut when a crossbow bolt flew into it.

Vela's palms grew sweaty. The captain would have to rely on her. "I think so. He's the tall one in a full suit of armor with a cobra insignia. Can you see him?"

"Aye."

"I know him," Louris cut in from below. "He is called Lord Algol. As one of the main leaders of Mevol, he owns most of the slaves and land you might find in that accursed place."

"Well, well," a mocking voice shouted from outside just then. "The protectors of this place are not phantoms, after all. We found that out by a well-placed arrow. If you want your two men back, I suggest you surrender, whoever you are. You have scared off my men for far too long. I'm here to end it." At his last words, Algol smacked his gauntleted fist into the palm of his other hand.

"What makes you think we'll give up so easily, Algol?" called Wurren, his voice grim.

"I have your men, and you have no choice. It's easy to decide. All I want is the captain of this Watchman team, and I'll let the rest of you go free."

"You'll release everyone in my territory? Or will you capture the people you want?

"All your friends, Captain." The fiend sounded like he was smirking from behind his helmet.

"Will he keep his word, Father?"

"He will," the answer came quietly after a brief pause.

Wurren took a deep breath and his mind whirled.

"Don't do it!"

The yell came from outside. Vela watched a warrior silence Kappa with a vicious blow to his side from the handle of his battle ax.

"Very well," Wurren said. "I agree. I'll do it."

At these words, Vela tore down the stairs.

"No. Wurren, you can't. We can fight our way out of this. I know we can!" Ankaa rushed over to Wurren, imploring him to stay inside.

The commodore walked over and placed a hand on Wurren's stiff shoulders. "I heard your choice of words, Wurren. You make all Asteri proud by protecting your country."

"Captain, they can take me instead," Vela offered. She descended the last of the stairs in a few bounds.

"No, Vela. He asked for *me*. Keep Gliese out of trouble while I'm gone, Ankaa. Vela, see that the commodore gets back to the Command Center safely."

Anger whirled inside Vela, but both she and Ankaa snapped one last salute. "You can count on us, Captain."

Wurren's eyes glittered with unshed tears. "I know." He slowly set his bow, sword, and knives on the table. Ankaa saluted again and she opened the door.

Vela peered around her captain. The warlord, Algol, looked slightly disturbed by the confident figure standing before him. Apparently, he had expected a barrage of arrows, hence his ready shield. Or maybe he'd figured on a defeated figure who would reluctantly give himself up. Wurren's proud, assured stance clearing startled the Mevolen.

"Let my two men go first, Algol," Wurren demanded.

The haughty lord nodded to his men who pushed Kappa and Gliese towards the cabin. The lieutenant stumbled. Gliese grabbed his friend's arm to keep the older Watchman upright. Kappa held his arm tightly, but blood seeped through his fingers, staining them red.

Wurren met them halfway to Algol. He rested his hands on their shoulders for a second before saying, "Kappa, let one of the girls take care of your arm. Gliese, don't cause too much trouble."

Then the captain of the Phoenix team walked away… just like that.

Chapter Seven

"Why did he do it?" Gliese still couldn't seem to believe Wurren had walked away.

The Phoenix Watchmen sat around in the main room discussing the new problem that had been thrown into their faces. Kappa was eager to go after the slave band and could hardly sit still. Vela hadn't seen him this agitated before. But it was understandable. From what Ankaa had told her, Kappa and Wurren were best friends. They would sacrifice their lives for one another.

"He had no choice, Kappa. Hold still," Ankaa growled when her patient moved again.

"It feels like you're digging into my arm with a burning-hot piece of metal," he retorted. "You could be a little gentler."

"If you didn't move then it might not hurt as much."

"We have to go after him," Gliese insisted from his place near the dying fire.

"Vela still needs to carry out the last command Wurren gave her," Ankaa argued. "Escorting Commodore Louris home might take a few days. That will give Kappa's arm time to heal. *Then* we can rescue Wurren." The young woman put the finishing touches on a bandage covering the arrow wound.

"Thanks, Ankaa," said Kappa.

"We'd better get going, Commodore." Vela rose from her seat, glad that the arguing was over. "I want to get you back as quickly as possible. No telling if Algol will come back for the rest of us."

"Aye, sir, you might want to leave soon," Gliese agreed, for which Vela was thankful. It felt wrong to tell the commodore what to do.

"I will," Louris said. "When I get back, I'll pull other Watchmen from their posts to cover for your team while you go after Wurren."

Ankaa gasped. "You mean we have permission to go, sir?"

"Aye, and if you need anything, just let me know."

Half an hour later, Vela and Commodore Louris started back to the Command Center. Vela enjoyed this journey much more than her first trip.

Vela took a deep breath of the clean air and Louris smiled. "Enjoying the rain free travelling this time?"

She nodded. "Aye, sir. It was a little miserable last time."

"Aye," Louris agreed. "How are you liking your new team? Are they accepting you? I know it can be hard at first."

Vela shrugged. "Sometimes I feel like they degrade me because I don't know basic stuff like horse riding. Ankaa is my friend now, but the others aren't as welcoming."

Louris' horse pranced uncertainly when he squeezed the reins without knowing it. "They've been through some difficult experiences with an apprentice. Give them time."

"Wurren told me a bit of what happened." Vela played with her cloak tie. "What was the apprentice like?"

Commodore Louris took a deep breath and let it whoosh out. "He was a handful, but in a good way. One of the best Watchmen I've seen. Wurren and him had a special relationship. It devastated him when—it happened."

Back at the Command Center, Louris sent messengers to the teams of the Dragons, Scorpions, and Bears. Each team promised to contribute two people to come to the Command Center and then on to the Phoenix base. Vela would accompany them. Once at the base, the temporary team would learn how things worked at the Phoenix base. After that, the rescue team would head out after Wurren.

Three days later, six well-trained Watchmen waited downstairs for Vela. She shyly descended the stairs behind Commodore Louris so as not to be seen at once. However, she could observe all the Watchmen.

"You called for us, sir?" one of the Dragon members asked.

"Aye. The Mevolens have captured a good friend of mine. You probably have not heard of him, but his name is Wurren. He gave himself to the raiders in order to free his team and me from the clutches of Lord Algol. You are going to follow this young lady, Vela, back to the Phoenix base and protect the area until their team returns. Any questions?"

"Where is their team going?" By the looks of the young man, Vela could tell he was from the Bear team.

"Into Mevolen territory to rescue Captain Wurren. I'll leave you to get acquainted. You leave first thing tomorrow morning." Louris left. As soon as he did, the Watchmen relaxed.

"You know my name. But what are your names?" Vela asked, still a little shy.

From the Dragons came Altais and Etamen. The Scorpions had sent Shaula and Lesath, and from the Bears came Alioth and Merak. All were men except Shaula, who seemed quite at home in the group.

"How did your captain get caught?" asked Lesath as the Watchmen sat around a table.

"He didn't 'get caught.' We were surrounded by fifty Mevolen soldiers and Lord Algol held two of our team captive. Not to mention, we had to protect the commodore. Wurren gave himself up so the rest of us could go free. My last command was to escort the commodore safely back here."

"That gesture is the mark of a true captain," Etamen put in.

"Why was Commodore Louris at your base?" Shaula asked. She looked curious.

Vela knew she didn't mean any harm, but that subject was confidential. "I don't know if I'm allowed to talk about it," she said then changed the subject. "You'll need a captain when the rest of the team and I leave. Have you talked about it at all?"

The other Watchmen looked at each other. "Not really." Altais shrugged. "But I think it should be one of the Bear Watchmen. From what the letter said, they live in a similar terrain."

Everyone looked at Alioth and Merak.

"I just graduated." Merak held up his hands. "It should be Alioth."

"Looks like you're the captain then, Alioth." Lesath grinned.

After all the bad things that had happened recently, it was a relief for Vela to talk to the replacement crew. She started to relax at their nonchalant attitudes.

The next day, the seven Watchmen started their two-day journey back to Phoenix territory. Many villagers and farmers watched the large group, clearly wary. Groups of Watchmen as large as this often-meant trouble.

They spent the night underneath a large tree with their horses nearby. Vela watched Alioth assert his new position and issue duties to all the Watchmen. "I'll take the first watch," she offered.

Alioth nodded. "Accepted. Thank you for offering."

From her place twenty paces from the campsite, Vela watched as Merak started a fire to roast a few plump quail, while the other Watchmen performed menial tasks around the camp. Some set up small shelters in case dew fell in the morning; others made bread for supper. A few just sat around and talked.

Vela took one of her irregular trips around the camp and stopped at another place to keep watch. Her thoughts turned to Wurren. Although he had given her the cold shoulder for a while, he'd proven that he cared when he gave himself up. *I wonder if he's all right.*

Her mind drifted. She shook herself awake and cleared her head. Then she rose and approached Alioth. "It's clear on all sides," she reported and sat down to eat with her companions. The night passed with no interruptions.

When they approached the cabin two days later, Ankaa, Kappa, and Gliese were waiting for them at the door. Kappa still wore a bandage on his arm. Vela waved and greeted her fellow Watchmen. "Hello!"

Dismounting, Vela and the others unsaddled their horses, grabbed their saddlebags, and turned their mounts loose in the field. Then they headed for the cabin.

Kappa stepped forward. "Welcome. I'm Kappa, and this is Ankaa and Gliese." He pointed them out. "We are the Phoenix team and we're grateful you came to help." He motioned them inside with his good arm.

"You are actually real?" Merak asked incredulously. His eyes grew large in wonder.

Ankaa turned away to hide her smile.

Vela shook her head and muttered, "Legends," as if she had never thought that way before.

"Gliese?" Altais stared for a second before shaking his head. "I didn't recognize you at first."

Gliese and Altais embraced and Etamen shook the Phoenix Watchman's hand. "Nice to see you again, Gliese."

"Kappa, these are some of my mentors from the Dragons!" Gliese exclaimed, turning to his friend.

Kappa inclined his head to the Watchmen. "Please, come with me." He led them inside.

"This cabin is exactly like ours back home," Etamen said inspecting the place.

"All the Watchmen bases are the same except for minor adjustments due to terrain," Ankaa put in. She leaned against the wall.

"Who's going to be in command while we're away?" asked Kappa.

Everyone looked at Alioth.

"That's me." He sighed.

"Do you have any experience, Alioth?" Kappa pressed him.

"Only a little. I just recently became a captain back home."

"Congratulations are in order, I'm sure." A hint of a smile flicked across Kappa's face. "I can give you a little help and a few tips on the terrain."

"Thanks."

"When is your team leaving?" Lesath had been quiet so far, but he piped up to ask his question.

Kappa started to answer, but Ankaa cut him off. "When Kappa's arm heals. Most likely in a few days."

He sent a deadly glare at her. "Gliese, could you please show them upstairs to their rooms?"

"Aye. Follow me." Gliese led the newcomers up the stairs.

Kappa sank down into a chair.

"Ankaa, I was planning to leave tomorrow. I thought I told you that." He glared at her again.

She smirked. "We're not leaving until you can handle your bow and maybe a sword. You would be useless if you can't handle your weapons." She crossed her arms, leaned against the wall again, and gave Kappa an admonishing look.

Vela snickered.

"I can be the brains," he began then paused at Ankaa's firm look. "Fine. But we aren't staying more than a few days."

"Good." Vela sighed. "It'll give me time to rest."

"We still have to pack," Ankaa reminded her.

"I can do that the hour before we leave." Vela waved it away. "I rode for several days straight, and you don't even let me rest."

"Get used to it," the lieutenant, Kappa barked. "We have harder work ahead. However, you have several free hours before supper."

A bolt of pain shot through Vela's heart as she tried to ignore his brusque tone. "See you later." She met Gliese and Shaula on the way down.

"Hey, Vela," Gliese said. "I was thinking that Shaula could use the room you and Ankaa share when we're gone."

"That's fine. Come with me, Shaula." Vela beckoned to the young woman, led her to the small room she shared with Ankaa, and showed her where she could set her bags.

"It's not much, but I hope you like it."

"I didn't know the Phoenix team was real until we got to the Command Center," Shaula said as she sat on the edge of a bed.

"Neither did I," Vela confessed. "Only, I didn't start out as well as you did. I think I might have insulted the Captain Wurren."

Shaula's eyes widened. "Oops. Not a great way to start out."

"I know, right?" Vela's eyelids drooped. "I'm exhausted, so would you mind if I could sleep?"

"I can go. See you later, Vela."

With that, the young Watchman was finally left in peace.

———▶———

Wurren slammed against a tree, the rough bark cutting into his cheek. Blood trickled from a cut on his face and he hit the ground with a grunt. It was finally getting dark. They had been on the trail all day, and the Mevolens had made sure it was very 'comfortable' for the Phoenix captain. When he had stepped away from the cabin yesterday, the raiders had lost no time binding him hand and foot. Then they threw him over a horse.

Wurren tried to duck a sudden kick aimed at his face. *Lord Algol certainly doesn't stop his men from harassing me. Not that I want to be protected by him.* Lying in the snow, he shivered. *Early winter.* It was getting colder and snow blanketed the area, but the group had yet to pass the peak of the mountain pass. Wurren's cloak helped only a little to preserve warmth. Little by little, the snow was sucking the warmth from his body.

A few men set up a tent for Lord Algol, while the others settled themselves on the ground. It grew dark. The

Mevolens ate handfuls of dried food they produced from their bags. No one offered anything to Wurren. He sat with his back against a tree. Sentinels were set and the rest of the men lay down without a word.

A long, cold hour later, Wurren noticed movement near the middle of the camp. The thin slice of moon made it hard to discern where the movement had come from, but the shadowy figure picked its way through the mass of sleeping bodies towards him. Wurren's muscles tensed when the figure crouched beside him.

But instead of stabbing a knife into Wurren's side, the mysterious person pulled something out of his pouch. "It's not much, but it'll have to do," he whispered. The soft accent of a Mevolen soldier slipped through his voice though he spoke in rough Rothrias.

"Why are you helping me?" Wurren matched the person's tone.

"No questions. Just eat." The man helped the captive eat the small piece of salty, tough meat. Then he laid a thick blanket over Wurren's battered body and he crept away as silently as a snake.

When Wurren awoke, the soldiers were rising, and he thought he had dreamt about the mysterious visitor. The blanket was gone, but he still felt warm. Had it been a dream?

After a breakfast of dried fruits, of which Wurren got a little, the raiders and their captive started on their way. *I wonder how angry Algol would be if he found out he let Commodore Louris slip through his fingers.* This thought cheered Wurren as the horses slogged through the snow. He shook his head and kept his thoughts to himself.

"Do you have enough food packed for the journey, Vela?" Ankaa asked as she checked her own saddlebags.

"Aye."

"Extra cloak?"

"Aye."

"Medical kit?"

"Aye, Ankaa. I've gone through the list twice. Everything's there." Her friend's eyes twinkled, and Vela realized Ankaa had been pulling her leg.

Several days had passed since Vela led the replacement Watchmen to the base, and Kappa's arm was well enough to use now, though he still had a bandage on. The team was gathering everything they needed, ready to go.

"Where'd you pack the extra weapons, Gliese?" Ankaa asked.

"Over there." The young man jerked his head towards the saddlebags that would go on the packhorse. "Good idea for bringing Twilight as a pack horse. Wurren would miss him otherwise."

"Oh good. Ankaa didn't forget the maps." The eldest Watchman, Kappa, sent a grin in Ankaa's direction. Vela stifled a laugh at the look her friend gave Kappa. "Really, Ankaa. We won't leave anything important behind. Don't worry. Ready?"

Ankaa, looking anxious, rolled her eyes. "Yep. Let's get moving."

Kappa checked the sun before setting the pace and turning towards Mevol. The team fell into a protective traveling formation, and Vela felt uncertain where to go.

Where do I fit in? They were heading into an enemy country and must be prepared for anything.

With a quick gesture, Ankaa motioned Vela to ride on the left side of the group. Vela fell into line, a little hesitant. Ankaa smiled at her, but Gliese and Kappa didn't give Vela even a glance.

She ducked her head and sighed, feeling more disregarded than ever. But she kept her expression impassive.

Chapter Eight

When the Mevolen party stopped the next night, Lord Algol summoned Wurren before him. "When we get back to my lands, I'll make you regret the day you were born," he sneered.

"That will be hard," Wurren replied. "I don't know the day I was born; My father didn't think of that being important. Did you know, Algol, that the commodore was in the cabin when you came for your little visit?"

"No, he wasn't," Algol snapped. "You're lying, like all you disgusting Watchmen do."

"The Good Book says, 'Lying lips are an abomination to the Creator.' I don't lie. I knew you're a man of your word, so I asked protection for all my friends. No wait, you said all my friends wouldn't be harmed. Thank you for securing his safety."

A gauntleted fist was the price for Wurren's cavalier attitude. "You tricked me!" Algol screamed his rage and hit him again. His prisoner would have fallen over from the blows if no guards were holding him up.

Wurren didn't answer, but spit blood out of his mouth.

"When we get back, you will never come out of Mevol alive!" Algol sent a final kick at Wurren before stalking off angrily. The guards jerked him back to a tree and tied him up.

Wurren had watched the men that day. He saw no signs of compassion from any of them. A commotion on the trail sometime during the morning resulted in a Mevolen's injuries. But from his position, Wurren couldn't see what had happened.

That night, Lord Algol set a guard by Wurren, and the mysterious person didn't come around. The young captain tried to shrug his cloak around so that it would cover his body more and leaned against the tree. At least that was dry. A fit of shivering seized him.

Against his will, his eyes drooped shut.

"Do the Mevolens really think that nobody would be sent after the captain?" Vela asked incredulously.

"Don't get excited," Kappa replied. He crouched down next to the churned snow. The tracks from the Mevolen warband showed plainly in the snow, making the trail easy to follow. "They might have set a trap for us. If we follow where these trucks lead, we could walk directly into it."

Vela wasn't sure if Kappa was talking to himself or to the rest of them as he muttered in a low voice.

"Remind me to thank Algol when I see him," Gliese quipped.

"We could follow twenty paces to one side of the trail," Ankaa suggested.

"Aye," Kappa agreed. "Let's go. I want to catch up to the group before they put Wurren in some horrible slave camp." Leaping into the saddle, he counted twenty paces to the right, keeping the churned snow in sight.

Vela hoped it was far enough away to avoid falling into a trap. "Brrr, it's cold up here." She wrapped her cloak tighter around her shoulders. "Good thing we're just going through the pass instead of up over the mountains."

"Aye," Ankaa said. "And since the Mevolens spend so much time up here waiting for the villagers to let their guard down, they're used to the cold." She pulled up next to Vela and asked, "Do you have a feeling we're being watched?"

Vela nodded. "I look one way and feel like someone is staring at my back. But when I turn, no one is there."

"I wonder if the boys feel it."

Vela glanced at Gliese and Kappa riding just ahead of them. She sighed. "Kappa still doesn't seem to accept me. When will he think of me as one of the team?" She stared at the back of the lieutenant up ahead.

Ankaa shook her head. "He's still struggling. Besides Wurren, he was the closest to our old apprentice. Kappa will come around. Just wait and see."

A few hours later, Gliese motioned them to a stop in a secluded clearing surrounded by thick evergreens. "Think this is a good spot to make camp for the night, Kappa?"

"Aye, I think so. We didn't cover as many miles today as I had hoped, though." Rubbing his arm, Wurren's lieutenant dismounted.

"Let me have a look at your arm, Kappa. I *knew* we shouldn't have started a day early," exclaimed Ankaa.

Kappa backed away from the persistent healer-woman. "It can wait. Let's get camp set up first."

With one last threatening look over her shoulder, Ankaa dismounted. She and Gliese took off to gather wood for the fire.

Vela was left behind with Kappa to unpack the mounts. She pulled the saddlebags from the horses and handed one to Kappa before putting the other heavy ones in a pile.

Kappa took his bag to the far side of the clearing and turned his back to her. However, Vela could see him reading the contents of what looked like a well-worn letter. Even from this distance she could tell it was wrinkled from being unfolded and folded many times, and the edges were torn.

Vela watched Kappa scan the contents of the letter again for what might be the thousandth time before folding and returning it to the waterproof cylinder he carried in his bags.

Interesting, I wonder—

She quickly ducked her head when Kappa turned around.

He looked like he might speak to Vela but just then, a sharp cry made them both look up. They sprinted towards the noise and found Gliese rolling on the ground with a stranger, who held a knife.

One minute the knife lay inches away from Gliese's chest. The next minute, the stranger's arm was twisted behind his back. Kappa ran forward and locked the stranger's arms behind his back, allowing Gliese to get up and pry the knife from the man's hand.

Ankaa lay on the ground a few paces away, looking dazed but unharmed.

"Let me go!" the stranger demanded.

"After you try to kill my friends?" Kappa said. "I don't think so." He tightened his grip and the man yelped when Kappa accidentally touched a partially broken crossbow bolt lodged in his arm.

"I thought you were some of those filthy, un—"

Kappa raised an eyebrow.

The stranger glanced at the girls then stopped. "Sorry, ladies. I thought you were Mevolen."

"We're taking you back to camp," Kappa said. "Ankaa, Gliese, are you hurt?"

"We're fine," the two Watchmen growled in unison.

"Good. Finish gathering the wood and meet us back at camp. And keep a sharper eye out, please."

They snapped a salute and picked up the wood that had fallen during the fight.

"Vela, come with me."

Vela trailed along behind Kappa as he propelled the newcomer into their camp and made him sit down. "Can we do anything for your arm?"

His question seemed to catch the young captive off guard. His eyes narrowed into slits as he studied Kappa. "Why would you care? I'm your prisoner."

"Well, that looks like a nasty arrow wound." Kappa retrieved a bag from his horse.

The stranger reluctantly let Kappa have his arm, but watched like a hawk while the Watchman cut the crossbow bolt off near the wound. "I might need your help, Vela."

Vela joined Kappa. Unease swirling in her stomach. "How can I help?"

Kappa glanced up at her. "Hold his arm steady, please."

He must be beginning to realize that he needs my help. Her stomach settled down. "Sure."

Kappa had quite a time getting the stubborn bolt out. When it was out, he rubbed salve on the man's arm and wrapped it with a fresh bandage.

"Thank you. But if you're not Mevolen, who are you?"

"We are Watchmen from Asteri, right across the border from Mevol. Have you heard of us?"

A frightened look flitted across the young man's face. "I have."

"What's your name?" Kappa asked. "And why did you have a Mevolen crossbow bolt in your arm?"

Vela twirled the arrow in her hands, examining it, while Kappa conversed with their guest.

The arrow was made of ash wood. Patterns and circles painted in bright red covered the shaft. From her time on the sea where bows were common during sea fights, Vela could tell it was a Mevolen crossbow bolt.

"My name is Heplar," the man said. "A war band of Mevolens passed through a week ago, and I tried to cause some chaos. One of them is a better shot than usual and got me in the arm."

Curious, Vela thought. "Why were you troubling the war band, Heplar?"

He shrugged. "It's what I do. It looked like they had a feisty prisoner with them." Heplar examined the bandage that Kappa had wrapped around his arm and nodded in satisfaction.

"That must be the band we're looking for!" Kappa exclaimed. Turning quickly to the young man he asked, "Were there any rear guards?"

Heplar shook his head. "No. They seemed in quite a hurry. Why do you ask? And why are you so interested in this war band?"

"Lord Algol was leading that band," Kappa explained. "He took a good friend of ours. We need to catch up with them and rescue him preferably before they put him in a slave camp." He stood and started pacing.

"Lord Algol? Are you sure?" Heplar shook his head in response to his own question. "No, Lord Algol never goes out on petty raids."

"He did this time. I saw him." Kappa waved at Vela. "We all did."

The quiet response made Heplar look up. His face showed concern. "Then I pity your friend. If he's a target for Lord Algol, he won't be treated well."

"Uh, Kappa?" Vela asked slowly, wondering if he would answer.

There was a pause before he asked, "Aye?"

"Shouldn't Gliese and Ankaa be back by now?"

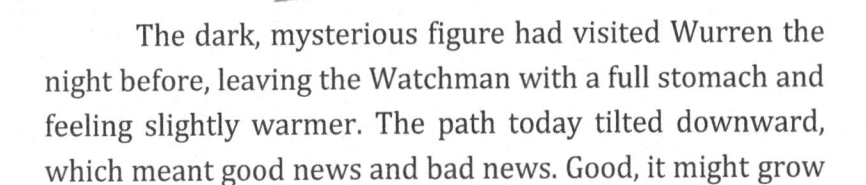

The dark, mysterious figure had visited Wurren the night before, leaving the Watchman with a full stomach and feeling slightly warmer. The path today tilted downward, which meant good news and bad news. Good, it might grow warmer. Bad, every step drew Wurren closer to certain, slow death.

All the Mevolens, especially Algol, seemed angrier than usual, due to an event earlier this morning. The warrior who had been injured a week ago had died. And who else would they take their anger out on but Wurren?

This morning, a guard purposely tripped him. He fell face forward into the melting snow. Then another, younger-looking guard, landed a kick into the Watchman's side when he walked past the prone prisoner. Someone prodded the horse Wurren was tied to, and it surged forward, dragging him through the snow.

It took a little maneuvering, but Wurren dragged a knee under himself and raised his drenched face above the snow for a deep breath. He gulped the cold air and staggered all the way to his feet, hurrying his steps to catch up with the horse.

Chapter Nine

"Rattlesnakes and scorpions!" Kappa exclaimed. "I forgot all about them!"

Vela jumped, startled at the Watchman's words.

He settled a black gaze on Heplar. "Do you know anything? Was anyone with you?"

When Heplar didn't answer, Kappa took one stride. His dirk hissed from its leather scabbard, coming to rest within an inch of the captive's neck.

"No one was with me!" Heplar insisted. "I really don't know what happened to your friends." His eyes darted to the blade that hovered only millimeters away.

"You'd better not have anything to do with it," Kappa growled. He stood and returned the dirk to its scabbard. "We've got to find them."

"I'll stay here with Heplar," Vela volunteered.

Kappa shook his head. "No more splitting up. We stay together from now on. Get up, Heplar."

The young captive rose carefully, hampered by his bandaged arm.

"This way." Kappa jerked his head in the direction the wood gatherers should have come.

Kappa led, followed by Heplar and Vela.

The area where the Watchmen had first met Heplar was almost in sight when Vela caught a flash out of the corner of her eye. She ducked and whipped out her sword, holding it between herself and the light-haired young man standing in front of her. He also held a sword.

The stranger wore a long black cloak with the cowl up. A longbow hung over his shoulders. He glared at her through glacier-colored eyes before executing a horizontal slice.

Vela blocked the attack and countered with a blow of her own. "Kappa!" She shot a glance at her fellow Watchman.

"I've got my own problems," Kappa shot back. He had drawn his sword even faster than Vela and now faced his opponent. The young, brown-eyed woman carried a satchel slung over one shoulder. Her clothes were a little frayed but overall in good condition. She held a stout staff in an offensive position in front and between the two warriors.

Vela saw all of this in the fraction of a moment before her own opponent attacked.

The young man lunged. He brought his arm back and forward. Vela saw a blur, then a small branch slapped her arm. She gasped at the sharp, stinging pain and dropped her sword. Her opponent brought his blade up into a ready position, waiting to strike at the first movement she made.

Vela didn't move. She watched Kappa who was eyeing the woman warily, looking for an opening. She stepped back and brought her staff up to her mouth and blew. There was a small whooshing sound.

Kappa ducked his head to one side to avoid the dart. With one hand, he grabbed the woman's staff and twisted it from her hands.

She let go, drew a short sword, and prepared to attack.

"Rena, Deyan! Stop! I'm fine."

At Heplar's call, the cloaked attacker stopped advancing on an unarmed Vela. He stepped back saying. "Heplar, we came looking for you after you didn't return several days ago. Were these people holding you up?"

"No, no. They took a Mevolen arrow out of my arm and bandaged it. We're looking for their two friends."

"Oh, *those* two." Deyan nodded in understanding while eyeing the Watchmen. "Follow me."

Vela sent one last look at the young man, Deyan, before grabbing her sword from the ground. She followed him, while rubbing her arm and wondering if they were walking straight into a trap. She raised an eyebrow at Kappa in an unspoken question but he didn't look at her. Almost like he was trying to avoid her gaze.

Vela's eyebrows shot up in surprise a few minutes later when the two strangers showed them their companions. Ankaa and Gliese lay unconscious and tied to a tree. How had two Phoenix Watchmen been overpowered, disarmed, and bound so easily?

Nearby, two other black cloaked people waited. They raised their loaded longbows when they saw Kappa and Vela.

Vela's heart jumped into her throat.

"Relax, Alek," Deyan ordered. "You too, Ralen. They're here for those two." He waved a casual hand toward the unconscious Watchmen.

"Aye," Kappa said. "We'll take them and be on our way." He never took his hand off the hilt of his sword.

"Then you'll stab us in the back." The one called Alek glared hard at them through icy blue eyes. "We know your type."

"We're just passing through," Kappa argued between clenched teeth. "The less time spent in one place the better. We need to catch up to a Mevolen war band."

"Aye," Heplar put in. "They're trying to free one of their friends from the clutches of Lord Algol. They say they saw him in the war band."

"Really? Where are you from?" Rena asked, curiosity in her voice.

"We are from Asteri," Kappa replied.

"Very well." Alek slowly lowered his bow.

"Anyway," Heplar said. "They helped me and—"

"What?" Ankaa stirred in the middle of Heplar's sentence. "Where am I?" She looked around in confusion before trying to wiggle free.

"Ankaa, what have I told you about watching your back?" Kappa sounded serious, but Vela grinned. He was joking, at least a little.

"I'm tied up and have a pounding headache. We're surrounded by potential enemies, and you still find time to chastise me?"

"Aye."

"Great."

"Could we please have our friends back?" Vela asked frowning. Shouldn't Gliese be awake by now?

"Maybe, if you first tell us why your friend is so important that four Watchmen are going after him." Ralen crossed his arms. His brown eyes watched intently, as if to calculate their reaction.

Kappa hesitated then spoke. "We're Watchmen, and the person they took was our captain. We are going to get him back."

"What team are you from?" Deyan threw another question at him.

"Phoenix," Ankaa answered.

Nervous looks came over the strangers' faces at Ankaa's words.

Kappa shot Ankaa a look, and she didn't say anything more.

"That means that you're phant—"

"Sorry to keep cutting off your sentences, Heplar," Vela burst out, "but we're *not* phantoms."

"Give us proof." Alek eyed them, and his hand moved a little towards his quiver.

Sighing, Kappa pushed up his shirt sleeve to reveal a blood-stained bandage. A very un-phantom sort of wound. Did phantoms bleed? Of course not! He snorted his impatience.

Before the strangers could react, Ankaa shouted from her spot under the tree. "You've gone and opened your wound *again*! I told you to take it easy."

Vela bit back a grin at Ankaa's furious outburst.

"I can take care of that for you." Rena opened the flap on her bag and stepped forward.

"No, it's fine," Kappa snapped. "We've got supplies back at our camp." The Watchman pulled his sleeve down again and shook his head.

"No more excuses," Ankaa said. "The longer you complain, the more blood you lose and the weaker you get." She jerked her head at a nearby rock. "Sit down and at least have her look at it."

"Just do it, Kappa," Vela encouraged him. "You'll be fine."

Deyan pulled out a knife and cut the ropes that held Ankaa to the tree. Then he cut Gliese's ropes. He had not yet awakened.

"I guess I hit him a little too hard in the head," Alek said sheepishly.

"He'll come around." Ankaa took a leather water bottle from the nearby pile of confiscated weapons and poured the contents on her friend's head.

Gliese came awake sputtering and Ankaa smirked. "Told ya."

"Ankaa," he growled as he brushed wet hair from his eyes.

"We never were properly introduced," Deyan said. "I'm Deyan. You've met Heplar, Rena, Ralen, and Alek."

"Nice to meet you. Although I wish it were under better circumstances. I'm Kappa. These are Vela, Ankaa, and Gliese."

"Would you like to camp with us? We hardly ever get visitors. The ones we do get are Mevolen, and we aren't on friendly terms with them."

Kappa seemed to consider Ralen's offer. "Maybe. We're not used to joining other groups when traveling, however."

Vela felt his gaze land on her and the other Watchmen.

Gliese held up a hand. "Don't look at me, Kappa. You're the leader. I'll let you make all the hard decisions." He stretched and rubbed his wrists to get the circulation back. "My head hurts."

"All right then," Kappa decided. "But only for tonight."

Rena finished wrapping a clean bandage around his arm and put her bag away. Turning to thank her, Kappa opened his mouth, but no words came out. A slight flush filled Rena's cheeks and she broke eye contact.

"Ankaa and I can fetch our supplies from camp," Gliese volunteered.

Kappa shook his head. "No. You and Ankaa aren't going anywhere together if you can't be aware of your surroundings."

Gliese flushed at the reprimand.

"Vela will go with you and see to it that you stay out of trouble," Kappa ordered.

Vela felt surprise written all over her face, but she didn't say a word.

"I'll show them the way." Ralen stood up from his spot on a fallen log.

Returning to their camp, Gliese and Vela made sure everything was packed onto the horses and led them back to the new camp, with Ralen's navigation help. The mysterious young man was quiet and only talked when needed. However, he appeared observant.

Back with the others, they made a small fire and ate. The older Watchmen made small talk with their new friends, but Vela noticed they didn't say much about their mission, jobs, home, or Asteri in general.

When they bedded down for the night, Ankaa whispered, "So, are we keeping watch tonight?"

"Aye," came Kappa's low reply. "Just don't make it noticeable."

When Vela's turn came around, she stuffed some bags under a blanket to make it look like she was still sleeping. Without making a sound, she sneaked off to the trees where she could watch the camp from the shadows.

The night dragged on. Vela yawned and nearly decided to go back to bed when she heard the slightest whisper of a noise. Two—no four—dark figures slipped one by one into the nearby woods. Stepping carefully, Vela followed. *What are these people up to?*

"When do we tell them?"

Vela froze and slipped behind the bushes. She strained her ears to catch their conversation.

"We don't need to tell them anything," came a hushed reply.

"But they were nice to Heplar. Shouldn't we tell them the truth?"

"They are *Watchmen*, Rena. They kill Mevolens like us. They wouldn't care or believe that we ran away from the army."

Rena pouted. "I still think we should tell them."

"If you want to stay alive, you'll listen to me," Deyan said. "We don't tell them."

Rena's silence showed she must have been contemplating Deyan's point.

Vela couldn't believe it. *These young people are from the Mevolen army? No wonder they're afraid of us.* This was news Kappa should hear at once. She crept back to camp and shook Kappa's shoulder. "Kappa, wake up."

He muttered a low groan and sat up. "My turn for watch already?"

"No. I have news. They crept away into the forest, all except Heplar. I heard them talking. They're from the Mevolen army."

Kappa sucked in a breath. "Are you sure?"

"Aye. Rena wants to tell us, but Deyan refused. He's clearly their leader."

Kappa nodded and pressed a finger to his lips. "Rouse the others, but do it *quietly*."

"Aye, sir."

When Deyan, Rena, Ralen, and Alek slunk back into camp sometime later, the four Phoenix Watchmen were wide awake. Kappa wasted no time but got straight to the point. "What are you not telling us, Deyan?" He crossed his arms.

"I don't know what you're talking about." Deyan returned to his sleeping mat and sat down. His hand fell behind his back, out of sight.

He's probably clenching the handle of his sword, Vela thought.

"Sneaking off in the middle of the night with three of your friends?" Gliese challenged. "No, not suspicious at all. What's going on?" Even the team's prankster sounded dead serious tonight.

"We have to tell you something," Rena announced.

"Rena, silence!" Ralen hissed.

"We're Mevolen," Rena went on, ignoring Ralen. "The boys escaped from the Mevolen army. Since I'm Ralen's sister, I came too. We've hidden out in these woods for two years now." Her honesty received dark looks from her brother and her friends.

"You're going to get us killed," muttered Alek out of the corner of his mouth.

"Why would we kill you?" Ankaa asked. "Watchmen protect Asteri. We don't kill every Mevolen we see. May I ask why you ran away from the army?"

"The army was getting ready to attack Asteri," Deyan explained. "Rena didn't want Ralen killed, so we all escaped together. We hunt for food and attack Mevolen war bands. You Watchmen have never come across the border, except one time a year ago."

The Phoenix team grew silent, as if remembering that terrible few days.

Vela jumped in. "If we both detest the Mevolen warbands, then we're not enemies." She turned to Kappa. "Right, Kappa?"

"Aye, Vela. We're mutual allies. Believe it or not, we might need your help getting our captain out. Will you join us?"

Relieved faces showed in the dim darkness of morning. They looked at each other then back at Kappa. "Aye, we'll join you," Deyan said.

"I need to warn you," Kappa said, "That if you join us, you must obey my orders."

Deyan nodded then turned to his friends. "It's almost morning. We might want to get ready to leave."

"We're going *back*?" Rena looked frightened.

"The friend of our new friends is in trouble. We can help him and pay Lord Algol a visit at the same time."

The small band packed up quickly, but they soon discovered a problem. The Watchmen owned the only horses. "I guess we could double up," Kappa suggested. "You do know how to ride, right?"

"Aye, all except Rena." Deyan glanced at the young woman.

"She can ride with me." Ankaa held her hand.

Gliese smiled and helped Alek up onto the saddle behind him while Kappa offered Deyan a ride on his horse. Vela offered for Heplar to ride behind her and Ankaa took Ralen over to Twilight.

"You can ride our packhorse by yourself," Ankaa said. "If you feel comfortable with that."

Ralen nodded his thanks and patted Twilight's flank gently before taking the reins from her.

Once on the trail, Vela pulled up next to Ankaa to talk. "Ankaa, will we tell the boys about the other mission? I have no clue what is written in there—"

Ankaa shook her head. "We'll talk later. Wurren is the priority now."

Chapter Ten

The Mevolen war band had arrived at the main part of Mevol, at least from what Wurren could make out. This was where most of the houses, slave camps, and castles were.

As the band moved its way slowly next to long, green fields, Wurren watched the slaves work under the hot sun. They wore ragged clothing that was either several sizes too big or too small. Rarely did their clothes fit properly.

Just then, a slave collapsed from the unbearable weight of a bag of cotton. In the blink of an eye, an overseer stood over the slave, whipping him mercilessly. He paid no heed to the poor boy's cries for mercy.

From studying the tactics of Mevol, Wurren knew that the fields grew mostly cotton, corn, and wheat, along with a few woodlots. A set of fields usually consisted of each type of agriculture. In turn, each set of fields was put under the leadership—or more often—the tyranny of a minor Mevolen lord. The more powerful lords owned more fields, to which the minor lords paid tribute to keep from being overrun and taken over.

For two weeks, this scenery passed in front of Wurren. He didn't see much variation to the endless fields, and his heart fell when he learned how many slaves the Mevolens had captured on their raids. Even with the Watchmen's hard work protecting Asteri, the Mevolens managed to steal their slaves from somewhere.

Their destination appeared to be a tall, dark castle overlooking a broad valley of fields, rivers, and farms. The evil lord's banner hung limply from the battlements in the heat of the day: a yellow cobra, poised to strike on a blood-red field.

Before they entered the castle, Algol waved a hand at Wurren and said, "Take him to Camp Twelve."

"Is he that dangerous, my lord?" one of the warriors asked in the Meveli language.

"Get moving before I have your heads," snarled the lord.

Ten men scurried away, heads bowed, leading the horse that Wurren lay across. It was obvious they feared their lord to a great extent.

Camp Twelve? Wurren's pulse quickened. When he was young he had heard rumors that Camp Twelve was reserved for the worst slaves, the ones that rebelled at the plantations or had a flighty nature. *Punishments are severe here in Mevol,* he mused.

The guards led Wurren farther down the road until Camp Twelve came into view. As they passed through the gate, Wurren kept his eyes open. What was he in for?

The Camp was constructed of half a dozen stone buildings, all of them put together inside a stone enclosure. Several people carrying pots and wearing aprons bustled around a small building that must be the kitchen. Not far away, a couple of barrack-looking buildings stood.

Across the compound stood another building, one that had several picks and shovels standing outside. *That must be a tool house.* The last building was small. A dozen slaves covered in soot and dragging their feet were just coming out of that place.

A guard pulled Wurren roughly off the horse and onto his feet. Weak and exhausted, the Phoenix captain nearly collapsed. His legs felt useless and were wobbly from spending the last two days on the back of that horse.

"Move," the guard ordered. He pushed the prisoner towards the barracks.

His legs still a little weak, Wurren stumbled and fell. The rough, stone-covered ground made him groan as he landed. The guards began kicking him, shouting at him to get up. Finally, Wurren clamped his mouth shut and struggled to his feet.

A burly guard unlocked a door, pushed the captain into a large room, and slammed the door shut. *It would have helped if the guards had cut my ropes.* Wurren landed on the ground and rolled over so he could push himself up with his still bound hands.

Someone grasped his arm with a firm grip and helped him to his feet.

"Thanks," Wurren said to the older man.

"My pleasure. Name's Reng. Mind if I get those off for ya?" He motioned to Wurren's bound hands.

"No, thanks. I'm fine."

Not taking any chances with this stranger, Wurren sat down and moved his hands to where he could see the knots better in front of him. In the dim light, the young captain made out about thirteen men sitting on cots that lined the walls. They all stared at him.

"Hello," Wurren greeted them, but his words were met with silence.

"We're not used to newcomers," the older man said.

"What do you do here, Reng?" Wurren asked. He eyed the knots and started bending his fingers towards the ropes.

"We work in the mines. Terrible place it is."

"No wonder they put me in here," muttered Wurren. "Thought I couldn't escape."

"You think you can escape?" Reng burst out laughing.

Wurren cocked an eyebrow at his prison mate's uncontrollable laughter.

After a little bit, Reng contained himself and said, "When you are put in Camp Twelve, you don't come out alive."

A sigh escaped Wurren's lips. "Algol already told me that twice. I don't need to hear it from you too."

"You mean Lord Algol? You must have done something terrible to make him mad at you," Reng observed, scratching at his arm.

Probably has fleas. Wurren shuddered. Then he grinned. "Yeah. I foil Algol's raids, nothing serious." With a smirk, the Watchman pulled his hands apart, letting the ropes fall to the ground.

"You're a *Watchman*?" one of the men gasped.

"Aye. Algol finally got tired of me. Any of you from Asteri?"

"All of us," answered Reng.

"Good."

Wurren was then introduced to the other unfortunate prisoners.

That night, lying on the raised wooden platform they called a bed, he wondered, not for the first time, about his team. *Where are they? Are they alive? Will I ever see them again?*

The Phoenix Watchmen and their new friends traveled all day, resting only briefly to eat lunch before they were on their way once more. Kappa seemed content with the miles they covered that day. Perhaps they'd cut off a day of travel between them and the warband.

The riding arrangement was working well, but Twilight was not used to having Ralen on his back. Even now he continued to act skittishly.

Vela had watched in amusement the first time Ralen tried to mount Twilight. He had approached the horse ready to mount up, but just as he was about to do so, Twilight shied to the side and Ralen's foot missed the iron stirrup. When he finally sat on the Watchman's mount, Twilight stood stock still for a moment before bucking. Ralen adjusted quickly so he wouldn't be thrown, but the horse changed directions lightning fast and the young man fell to the ground.

Rena ran to help him up while Ankaa calmed Twilight. The horse snorted and looked at the stranger who had just tried to ride him. It was almost as if the horse was telling Ankaa that he despised this young man.

Ankaa rubbed Twilight's nose four times and then gently tapped Twilight's head right between his eyes. The stallion's ears flicked forward. He looked at Ralen once more before sidling over to him.

Ralen sent a confused look at Ankaa who nodded to Twilight.

"Sometimes our horses need a little encouragement to let strangers mount."

Ralen swung up and twitched the reins lightly. A pleased smile spread across his face at how quickly the Watchman's horse now responded to his movements.

That night, the group found a perfect spot near a stream to camp. Vela and Ankaa took the horses to one side, and Gliese and Alek went to collect firewood with their long knives. Shortly after they left, Ralen and Heplar seemed to agree on the perimeter watch. But Vela noticed that Ralen seemed reluctant to leave Rena, who was tending Kappa's arm. *Ralen and Rena seem close.*

Vela and Ankaa finished settling the horses. Vela had no problem hearing Kappa's and Deyan's discussion as they studied the maps.

"I'm glad I asked you to join us," Kappa said, bending over a map. "Out of the whole team here, only I know Meveli and even that knowledge isn't very extensive."

"We're done with the horses." Vela walked up. "I know Meveli."

Kappa's head shot up. "*What?* Why didn't you tell me?"

Shame heated Vela's face. She shrugged. "I don't know. My father once knew of a resistance in the forest of Mevol, made up entirely of escaped slaves. Maybe they can help us. He was close friends with their leader."

Kappa stared at her then shook his head. "You are full of surprises, Vela."

"What forest was it?" Deyan asked, leafing through several maps that were scattered around. He motioned Vela to look at the maps and point out the location.

"Melarin Forest, I think," she answered slowly.

"That's our next stop then."

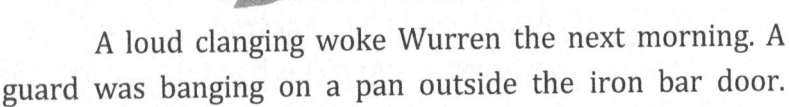

A loud clanging woke Wurren the next morning. A guard was banging on a pan outside the iron bar door. Groggily, Wurren sat up from his place on the raised wooden platform that served as a bed.

The men other stood, and Reng motioned Wurren over. "That-there door will open, and we'll go to breakfast, if you can call it that. Try to ignore the guards."

The door opened just then and the men filed through. Wurren followed and found two tables awaiting them. Benches lined the sides of one long table. The other table, small and square, held a pot of—

Wurren wrinkled his forehead. Oatmeal? *I'm not sure one can call it that, but maybe that's what it's supposed to be.* He took his place at the back of the line and waited while the men filled their bowls with the watery mush food. When Wurren's bowl was filled, he sniffed. It smelled burnt. He sat down and took a taste. Unappetizing, but he ate it anyway. *If I am to escape, I'll have to eat something.*

Wurren looked up. A walkway along the top of the stone walls encircled the eating area where guards stood watching the prisoners. Several guards threw nasty comments at the men and received silence for their troubles.

One guard appeared very young and quiet. He looked younger than Wurren. However, he wore the emblem of Algol—a yellow cobra on a blood-red field. *The boy's allegiance is clearly set. His age won't stop me from hurting him. I wouldn't want to kill him, but I will if I have to. I must be prepared to do what I need to do to get these men out safely.*

Wurren was barely scraping his bowl clean when one guard yelled, "Stand up, slaves. Time fer work."

The man to Wurren's immediate right stood and shook his fist at the guard. "Why don't you come down and make me?"

"No. Don't say that, Corsis. He'll beat you," Reng begged.

The guard laughed and disappeared through a doorway. A minute later he opened the gate and sauntered into the food room. Corsis' face was pale, but he stood his ground as the taunting guard drew close. The other slaves stood with their heads bowed in submission and the guard shoved a few slaves aside to approach Corsis. *Why don't they do something?* Wurren wondered.

"Smart mouthin' me, brat?" the guard asked in rough Rothrian. "I'll teach you!"

One powerful shove sent Corsis tumbling over the long table, scattering bowls and spoons. The slave dragged himself up and held his fists in a weak fighting position. Laughing again, the guard pulled a knife from his belt.

"I'll cut ou' yer insolent tongue and this will be settled," he said.

Wurren couldn't stand still for a moment longer. He jumped forward and kicked the guard's feet out from under him. The guard hit the ground with a thud and the knife flew through the air. It landed on a table with a clatter. Wurren dove for the knife but jerked to a stop at the bright blade hovering in front of his chest. And on the other end of the sword was the young guard.

"Foolish Asterian," he barked. "Know your place!"

With a twist of the wrist, the young guard let his blade draw blood. Wurren pressed a hand against his arm where the sword had sliced him, staining his fingers with blood.

"Now get to work! All of you!" the young guard shouted.

Most of the slaves fell over each other trying to get out the door. Only Wurren lagged behind to see if Corsis was alright. Corsis didn't meet the Watchman's eyes as he shuffled by. The cold gaze of the young guard followed Wurren out the door.

Reng matched his stride as they were herded towards a building. Guards hit, pushed, and heckled the men. Wurren clenched his fists and kept his mouth shut.

"That was a brave but rather fool-hardy thing you did back there," Reng whispered.

"Perks of my job," Wurren replied. He fumbled as another slave shoved a pickaxe into his arms.

The guards pointed at a small building Wurren had first noticed upon his arrival. The slaves crowded inside and formed into a line that headed down a pair of rickety stairs.

A faint glimmer of light revealed where a torch was settled in a niche in the wall. The next light source wasn't located for another twenty paces. The Watchman shuddered and drew a deep breath as he stepped down into the darkness. One of his worst fears when he was a little boy was being caught in a tight place with no way out. Down here, in the deep, dark depth of the earth, the horror of that feeling returned. He struggled to submerge the panic that was slowly but certainly rising.

Once they had passed through the tunnel's mouth, Reng pulled Wurren aside. "I pull carts, so you can help pull mine. It doesn't look like the guards have any special job for you yet and since you're our only hope for escape, we want to keep you alive. Come with me." The older man put aside Wurren's pickaxe and showed the captain a large cart that ran on wooden tracks down into the depths of the mine. "We go by each mining station and pick up a supply of coal. Then we push it up to the mouth of the tunnel and dump it on a big pile outside."

The rotten looking cart creaked as the uneven, wooden wheels grated against the tracks. Apparently, Reng had talked with the other unfortunate prisoners and they had decided to give Wurren one of the easiest jobs in the mine. The frequent stops fresh outside air calmed Wurren.

Little by little, he adjusted to the dark passageways in the bowels of the earth.

Chapter Eleven

Melarin Forest loomed large and dark against the bright blue sky that overlooked the traveling Watchmen and their friends. They sat a few yards away from the tree line and gazed at the foreboding sight.

The last two and a half weeks had passed in a blur of traveling, hiding from Mevolen warriors, and more traveling. Vela had struck up an easy friendship with Rena and Ralen and discovered she liked the siblings. Ralen was the quieter of the two, but Rena talked eagerly with her.

"Did your father ever say where the resistance hid out, Vela?" Ankaa didn't take her eyes off the dark shadows.

"No. They might all be dead by now, but it's worth a chance. If anyone knows where the captain is, those former slaves will know." Setting her chin in firm determination, Vela nudged her horse one step towards the forest. The others quickly accompanied her, though they gave cautious glances into the deep shadows.

Tall, leafy trees blocked most of the sunlight from reaching the forest floor, resulting in dark shadows covering the ground. A slight wind tossed Vela's hair and rustled the leaves, as if someone stalked them. The group constantly turned their heads at the new noises. Shadows danced eerily around them, making Vela feel as if a dozen dark warriors surrounded them.

Kappa stopped his horse and turned around. "I don't like this. Let's head back."

"No." Vela took a deep breath. "We need to find the captain. He could be hurt or sentenced to death. We can't leave him there, wherever he is."

The lieutenant locked gazes with Vela. "We can find him another way, one that doesn't involve this forest. Who knows what lies ahead? Maybe a trap, where we'll fall to our deaths. What help will we be to Wurren then? It's safer to find a different source of information than risk our lives on people who might not even be alive any longer."

"The Creator knows what's ahead," Vela countered. "He will keep us safe. I don't care if you leave, Kappa. I'm going on alone, even if none of you will come with me." To show that she meant what she said, Vela urged her horse forward.

Kappa put his horse, Dermen, in her path. "Fine, but let's dismount and walk ahead of the horses. It'll be safer." He slipped off his horse and led his mount behind him with his hand on the halter. The rest of the group followed suit.

Not too far along the trail, Rena's foot broke through the ground and into a deep hole. She gasped, waving her arms wildly.

Swiftly, Ankaa grabbed Rena's arm to save her but started falling too. Ankaa's horse, Valiant, leaped forward, allowing Ankaa's hand to grasp her saddle and regain her balance.

Ralen's shoulders sagged in relief when his sister stepped back, clearly shaken but okay.

"Let's see how big this hole is." Gliese grabbed a nearby branch and started tapping the ground.

As more and more branches and dirt caved in, the hole grew wider. The top of the hole had been covered with branches cut even with the ground. A light layer of dirt lay scattered on top, along with dead leaves and branches.

"A score of soldiers could fit inside this pit," Alek said with awe.

Picking their way carefully around the hole, the group continued, with Gliese and Alek in the lead. They had an unspoken agreement that everyone would take turns leading and scouting for more traps.

Gliese stopped suddenly and held up his hand. Everyone halted. Drawing a knife, he cut a string running over the faint trail they were following. Vela frowned as she heard the sound of a rope running through a pulley somewhere. With a crash, a large tree branch smashed into the earth a single stride in front of Gliese. He simply grinned.

The trees were too tall and grew too close together to determine sunset, so Kappa decided to make camp early. They lit no fire, and everyone ate dried food from their saddlebags.

The group stayed strangely quiet, as if the eerie forest had silenced them. After the meal, there wasn't much to do. No one seemed interested in talking, so they retired early. "I'll take the first watch," Alek volunteered.

The others got comfortable.

Then an owl cried, *whoo-hoo.* Another owl's cry drifted through the forest. Then, quicker than Vela could blink, at least forty dark-clothed people—all holding bows—surrounded the little group.

Vela, Ralen, Alek, and Heplar drew back their bow strings, while the rest drew their swords.

"What are you doing in our forest?" a raspy voice demanded.

"We're here to ask for your help," Kappa replied warily. "We were told that you could help us."

"We help no one," came the stout answer.

"Would you fight Algol?" Ankaa demanded.

"Aye, that we do gladly," the man said with a smirk.

"Then maybe we can work something out. Algol took our captain, and we want him back." Kappa lowered his sword.

"How did you hear about us?"

Kappa motioned Vela to speak. She stepped forward and said, "My father was a merchant in the Rothrian Sea. He knew your leader."

The man's mouth dropped open. "Your father is the merchant?"

"Was," Vela corrected. "He was murdered."

Several gasps and groans came from the men.

"I will help you," the first speaker said. "But who are these people with you?"

"They're the other members of my Watchmen group, as well as friends we met on the way."

The man glared hard at the group of young people before saying, "Come with me."

The strangers melted into the shadows to allow the Phoenix team and the Mevolens to follow the first man, their horses following close behind. Vela marveled at how these people moved through the forest like shadows.

The journey through the forest went quickly, but with the darkness surrounding her, Vela felt an ominous threat, though it was slight. After crossing a river on a fallen tree, they finally stopped near a clearing.

Pointing at Vela, the speaker said, "You come with me. The rest of you stay here."

Ankaa looked like she might object, but a look from Kappa kept her in check.

Someone had set up camp in this clearing. Several fire pits crackled and snapped, and weapons lay stacked in one corner. Two older men consulted a map near one of the fires in the middle of the clearing. They turned and watched the approaching people.

"Lider, sir. On patrol we ran across these people, who say they were looking for us." He waved at Vela. "This girl claims to be the merchant's daughter."

"Is that so?" Lider looked at Vela. "Then maybe you can tell me why he stopped visiting my house before I came to live here in these woods."

This man is their leader, Vela decided. Although he seemed older than a middle-aged man, he was straight-backed and tall. Lines on his face told of unnumerable hard decisions and countless hardships.

Vela closed her eyes to collect her thoughts then opened them and looked at Lider. "A couple years ago, our ship was attacked by Mevolen pirates in their warships. They captured my sister and me, but my mother and father were killed. The League of Watchmen rescued me, but my sister was taken. In my younger days, I often heard my father talk of you." She paused and ducked her head. "We need your help."

"I am sorry you had to go through that, Vela."

Her head jerked up. How did Lider know her name?

"Aye, your father was very proud of his two beautiful daughters. He talked of you often." He waved his arm to indicate those standing around him. "Your father is honored by these men, so much that they hardly dare to speak his name. Now, why do you need our help?"

Vela explained how Wurren had given himself to Algol in exchange for his friends and why they were going after him. Then she asked for his help again.

"Hmm," Lider considered. "If it's against Algol, we might consider it. Where are your friends? Bring them forward."

Vela beckoned to the others who slowly approached.

"There are none better than a team of Watchmen," Lider confessed after greeting them. "But where did you find these others?" His arm indicated the Mevolens.

"In a forest a day after we crossed the border," Vela answered.

"We have heard reports of activity in those woods," Lider said. "My scouts discovered that the troublemakers are Mevolen, and we don't like Mevolens in our camp."

Several men who seemed to be guards approached, swords drawn.

Gliese stepped forward. "With all respect sir, aye, our new friends are Mevolen. But they ran away from the army. Now, they harass the war-bands that travel through their territory. They have agreed to help us find our captain."

Lider glared hard at the Mevolens, as if he could see right through them. Then he relaxed and motioned his men to settle down. "Very well. If the Watchmen can trust these Mevolens, then we will too."

"Where do you think our captain has been taken?" Kappa asked.

"Camp Twelve," Lider replied with certainty. "That's where Algol puts the prisoners he doesn't like." He pressed a finger to a place on a nearby map.

Vela peeked over his shoulder. His finger rested on the part of Mevol farthest from Asteri. She sighed inwardly. *It's going to be a hard rescue.*

Reng and Wurren pulled coal carts the whole day. Besides a brief stop for the midday meal, they had no other breaks. A horn blared at sunset, signaling the end of the day. Wurren had held up well, but he limped out of the mine, completely worn out. Supper that night was a thin soup with small chunks of meat floating around. *Hardly a nutritious meal.*

After supper, Wurren lay on his bed weighing their chances of escape. The ever-present guard overlooking their quarters limited the prisoners' talk to useless subjects. But the men were so exhausted that even useless subjects were hardly spoken of.

The guard on duty tonight was the young man who injured Wurren this morning at breakfast, the quiet one that was good with his blade. He did not hurl terrible names at the prisoners, not as the other guards enjoyed doing.

As soon as the captain of the guard left the one young guard to his duties, the youth looked around then disappeared through a small doorway. Curious, Wurren watched from his bed as the guard reappeared with a length of rope and threw it over the wall.

The youth's noiseless motions reminded Wurren of a stealthy figure visiting him in the middle of the night. The guard slid down the rope and dropped to the ground with a soft *thunk*.

The prisoners sat up in surprise, mouths hanging open.

Wurren sat up, then stood, his muscles tensed and ready for a fight. Perhaps this guard wanted to finish what he had started earlier. Every nerve tingled.

Their eyes locked as the youth drew his knife. Wurren bent his knees and felt a flicker of regret about what he might do to the young guard.

The young guard put a finger to his lips, cautioning silence. Then he extended the knife to Wurren, hilt first. "You might need this." His voice was barely above a whisper. "Don't let any of the other guards see it."

Wurren relaxed, but he took the knife with hesitant confusion. "You're the one who helped me on the trail, aren't you?"

"Aye, but do not tell anyone." With a few bounds, he leaped halfway up the rope. He climbed over the wall, pulling the rope up behind him.

When the stranger had disappeared, Reng asked quietly, "What was that all about?"

"I have no idea, but I plan to find out."

"We can provide the distraction to get you in and out, but I don't have enough men for a full-scale attack." Lider, Kappa, and Deyan were examining a rough sketch of Camp Twelve and planning a rescue mission, while Vela and the rest of the Watchmen sat nearby listening.

Kappa bent over the map. "I don't think we need a full-on attack, just a big diversion."

"My scouts have seen a wooden side door at the opposite end of the camp. If that catches fire, it could draw a lot of attention," suggested Lider.

"Would it be big enough?" Deyan countered, scrutinizing the map. "There might still be guards in the barracks."

"Maybe we could manage a little more confusion." A smile crossed Lider's face. "I think this will work fine. Just let me talk out some details with the others."

Kappa turned to go, but Deyan's words stopped him. "We're coming with you."

The Watchman turned back to the Mevolen. "I will not let you risk your lives for someone you don't know. You said you would obey my orders. And the fewer that go, the better."

"Who we are risking our lives for is none of your concern," Deyan insisted. "It's one way we can get back at Lord Algol. You can use several more swords and bows. We can move almost as silently as you Watchmen."

Kappa's face clouded with a memory that seemed dark and sad. He shook his head. "No more innocent lives will be lost. Wurren would agree with me."

"I am no expert of Asteri, but I recall the Prince once said, 'There is no greater love than this, that one shall lay down his life for his friends,'" Deyan quoted. "That includes your captain."

"I can't believe you used an Asterian quote against me," fumed Kappa. He turned away to ponder the request. "He's not even from the same country," he muttered.

"We might need their help," prompted Gliese, who was sharpening his sword.

"Is *everyone* against me today?" the Watchman barked in exasperation.

"Pretty much," Ankaa added.

Vela smiled as she watched the exchange. *My opinion doesn't matter much.*

Kappa sighed deeply and turned to Deyan. "All right. You can come. But if I tell you to escape, then you do it."

"Aye, sir." Deyan saluted smartly and marched off to brief his friends.

Chapter Twelve

Camp Twelve was a four-day journey from Melarin Forest and there was still a lot of preparation work to be done. Weapons must be honed, food and equipment packed, and resistance fighters chosen.

In addition, Kappa told Vela he wanted to run her through some basic weapons maneuvers. The next day, he interrupted her while she was fletching arrows with Ralen. "Let's spar a bit, shall we?" He made it sound like she'd better not refuse.

I hope I don't bungle this, Vela thought. She drew her sword and followed Kappa to a clear spot in the trees. A sudden question popped into her head and she spouted it off without thinking.

"Why are you sparing with me now when you never did back at the cabin?" she blurted out.

Kappa frowned. "That is a personal question I won't answer. And I am not here to train you. I am here to assess your skills."

Vela melted a bit under his hard gaze before setting her fighting stance. Kappa drew his sword as well and lunged forward. Vela's mind screamed *"Block!"* And her muscles barely managed to react in time. Kappa's sword flashed again, darting towards her right arm.

She was so caught up in deflecting his attacks that Vela didn't know Kappa had tripped her till she was laying on her back in the dirt.

"I guess you haven't learned how to combine footwork into your swordsmanship yet," Kappa commented.

"I've only been training for a few months," Vela snapped back. "I shouldn't even be going on this mission. I'm only going because you can't find someone to babysit me."

"Sorry, I should've gone easier on you," apologized Kappa.

Vela blinked in surprise. *Kappa is apologizing to me?*

He shook his head. "And you're not going on the mission because we have to babysit you. You're going because you're a valuable part of this team."

"Says the person who's ignored my existence since I arrived." Scrambling to her feet, Vela dusted herself off and sheathed her sword with a crisp *snap*.

Kappa sighed. "All right. Let's move on with the assessment. Go get your bow and—let's say fifteen arrows."

When Vela returned, she found Kappa holding some wooden disks that he was tossing up and down experimentally.

"I'm going to trust that you have good enough aim not to hit me," he said straight-faced. "So I will throw this disk in the air and you shoot it before it touches the ground."

Vela nodded and drew several arrows from her quiver. Nocking the first one, she waited. The first disk snapped into the air and almost took her by surprise. But a split-second later, an arrow slammed into the disk. Kappa didn't hesitate and tossed another in the air, giving her little time to nock another arrow.

When disk after disk fell onto the ground with an arrow protruding from it, Kappa finally nodded. "You'll use your bow on this mission. Carry your sword with you though. Just in case of an emergency."

It was dark when they moved out. The resistance gave Deyan and his friends some horses they had liberated from the Mevolens. Lider estimated that it would take four full nights of travel for them to reach cover near the camp. A scout had gone ahead to clear the area. The diversion group consisted of Lider and his thirty men, while the Watchmen and others would penetrate the defenses.

Night traveling was difficult, especially with barely a moon to guide their steps. However, they must be stealthy so the Mevolens wouldn't expect anything. They were lucky that there were no rivers to cross, for it would have made for a treacherous crossing. Several creeks gave them a slight delay. The group scrambled for the hiding places as the sun topped the tall mountains in the west.

This day's hiding place was a large cavity hidden between two larger boulders on one side and a thick hedge on the other. Soft grass carpeted the ground, making the hideout a welcoming place to rest their heads. After making camp, Ralen motioned to Vela. When she joined him, he helped her stand on one of the surrounding rocks.

"There." He pointed. "Camp Twelve."

"We're so close," she whispered.

Fear crept into Vela's mind, but she quickly dismissed the thought. She couldn't be afraid. Wurren was held captive in that awful place. They must be strong to get him out. *I'm not going to back down now.*

"We can do it," Ralen assured her.

"Of course."

"I know we can."

Vela caught a trace of hesitation in his voice. She darted a glance in his direction, but he turned away. Perhaps she had missed his tone or misinterpreted the flicker of uncertainty in his eyes.

She hoped so.

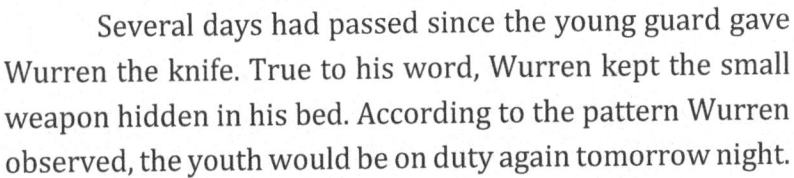

Several days had passed since the young guard gave Wurren the knife. True to his word, Wurren kept the small weapon hidden in his bed. According to the pattern Wurren observed, the youth would be on duty again tomorrow night.

Today, however, had not gone well. The guards had caught Wurren hauling a coal cart and decided to make him work harder, ordering him to handle a pickaxe for the rest of the day. His muscles had stopped aching a day ago, but this new work made them sore all over again. He collapsed into bed that night, exhausted.

While he slept, the resistance were fulfilling their plans. A few hours later, two resistance fighters sat next to a smokeless fire listening for their signal. An owl call broke the monotone of crickets droning on in the still night air. Then came a pause of exactly two seconds before another came. Nodding to each other, they put some arrows with oil-soaked rags wrapped around the shafts into the fire. The arrows flew straight and struck the door with muffled thuds. Flames leapt at the wood and devoured it. The two archers left the guards alone because the whole plan was to distract them and the louder the guards shouted, the better.

On the other side of the camp, Vela and the rest of the Phoenix team, along with Deyan and his friends, were ready to move. The wall in front of her was about twice as tall as herself. Cloaked in dark colors, the group waited until a commotion broke out.

Sudden shouts and yelling filled the silence right on cue.

Vela smiled inwardly. The archers' diversion had worked. Guards disappeared from the wall in a noisy tumult.

"Help your partner up and get over that wall," Kappa ordered.

Hurry, hurry! The thought raced through Vela's mind. Ankaa boosted her as high as she could reach. Vela's fingers curled over the top edge. Huffing and puffing, she clawed her way to the top. She secured a rope to a metal bracing and let it drop to her friend. Ankaa scurried up and joined her.

Not far away, the others repeated Vela's and Ankaa's climbing on various parts of the wall. Soon, the team was creeping along the top of the wall. Crouching low so as not to be seen, they dropped off the walkway and silently ducked into the long shadows of the barracks.

Gliese slipped up next to a door and fiddled with the lock for a moment before pushing against the door. It opened without a creak. No guards were in their quarters, so

Gliese waved a hand, and the invaders bounded up a flight of stairs.

Vela and the others easily spotted the wall that stretched above the prisoners' quarters. Ankaa, who was now in the lead, drew her sword. Vela sucked in a breath when she saw the guard. The guard jumped in surprise and drew his sword.

Too late. Ankaa flew forward and knocked his sword out of his hand. Then she sent him to the ground with a blow from her hilt. Gliese gagged and bound the guard. Deyan secured his rope to a supporting beam and dropped it over the wall. "Wurren?" he whispered hoarsely.

Down below, Wurren sat up groggily at the voice. Then he jumped out of his bed, clearly wide awake. "You made it!"

Vela's heart leaped. Wurren was here, and he sounded all right!

Wurren shook one of the other prisoners. "Reng," he whispered, "My team is here. Wake the others." He turned and met Kappa as his lieutenant slid down the rope. They clasped arms in greeting. Wurren's smile threatened to crack his face.

"Come on, Wurren," Kappa said. "We don't have much time."

"I want all of us to get out." Wurren motioned behind him to the other prisoners, who waited expectantly in the shadows.

Kappa started, thought, then nodded. "Of course. So long as everyone hurries." He and Wurren stood aside and motioned the other men to move quickly and quietly. Wurren grabbed the knife from his bed and took up the rear.

Before long, Wurren was reaching for the rope lifeline. He followed the others up the rope, nodding briefly at the smiles the Phoenix team sent in his direction. Then silently, they sped along.

Hurrying down the stairs, Gliese suddenly stopped. Wurren nearly rammed into him. "What—"

Finger to his lips, Gliese pointed at an open door. Vela, just behind Wurren, bit her lip. They had left that door closed.

"The guards won't wait all night. I suggest you get out of here fast," a new voice came from behind the group.

Deyan spun and drew his sword before executing a slice at the voice. A curved sword met his and flicked it away. A rasp of steel sounded as Wurren drew his knife and knocked away the arrow that Kappa had just released.

"Don't bother with me. You're wasting time. Get going." The guard sheathed his sword and pointed at the door.

Kappa was ready to shoot again, but Wurren put a hand on his shoulder. "Don't shoot. He's with us."

Deyan put his blade away and the Watchman lowered his bow, but both kept wary eyes on the guard.

"Come with us," the Phoenix captain offered the guard. "I know you don't want to stay here."

The young guard looked at the outstretched hand then at the ground. "You're right, I don't. But there's someone I can't leave behind who's held in Lord Algol's castle. I gave my word that I wouldn't leave without taking her with me."

Wurren nodded. "I respect that. Come with us, and we'll see what we can do." He stood waiting until the young guard nodded and joined them.

Groups of seven were created to scale the wall, with five prisoners and two rescuers in each group. That way, they could offer assistance for the weaker ex-prisoners.

"Who created the distraction, Vela?" Wurren asked in a whisper as they waited their turn to cross the wall. Crouched in the long grass, they stayed out of sight from the Mevolen guards, at least for the time being.

"Resistance fighters we found in Melarin Forest."

"And the other people you brought with you?"

"Friends we made on our way here. Their names are Deyan, Rena, Ralen, Alek, and Heplar. The boys were in the Mevolen army until they ran away, taking Ralen's sister Rena with them. They attack Mevolen war-bands heading from and returning to Mevol."

"You mean to say they're *Mevolen*?" Wurren's eyebrows shot up in surprise. "Why would they help us?"

"To get back at Algol," Vela answered simply. Then she closed her mouth and concentrated on not being caught.

Chapter Thirteen

Going back the way they came was the easy part. After sending a signal to Lider, the rescuers took the ex-prisoners back to the makeshift camp. To Wurren's relief, Kappa gave him his weapons back and a new cloak to replace the one that had been taken. Lider and his men returned with stories of how they had kept the guards busy with the fire and a good pounding with a makeshift battering ram.

Everyone was nervous about the young Mevolen guard. Everyone except Wurren, who knew how the young man had provided necessities both on the long road and also during his confinement.

Back at camp, the guard stayed aloof. He did not engage in conversion unless asked a direct question, which was rare. The team seemed to be holding him at arm's length, suspicious of any Mevolen, especially a prison guard. Finally, the Phoenix captain motioned him over to the edge of camp. It was time to learn some answers. "What's your name, boy?"

The guard fingered the red tabard that held Algol's emblem. "It's a long story and complicated."

Wurren gave him a smile. "I've got the time. Let's start with a simple question. Did you want to be in the army?"

"No!"

Startled by the youth's vehement answer, Wurren asked, "Who *are* you?"

Tears formed in the young man's eyes. "Don't you remember me, Wurren? I'm Gilian, your brother!"

Stunned, Wurren stared until it dawned on him. *His face! I knew he looked familiar, but the fuzz on his chin threw me off.*

He engulfed Gilian in a tight hug, tears springing from his eyes. "We thought you dead! After finding your mount, we tore the forest apart looking for you, but you had vanished."

"Wurren?" Kappa ventured.

Wurren spun around. His team and the rest of the group were looking at him and the Mevolen guard in confusion. "Come here!" he beckoned.

The team rushed over. "Is something wrong?" Gliese demanded, his hand going to his sword hilt.

"No!" Wurren shook his head, grinning. "Do you recognize this young man?"

Gilian took off his helmet revealing a shock of dark-brown hair. His green eyes twinkled.

Vela scrutinized him and shook her head. "I don't know him."

Kappa gasped and staggered backwards. "This is impossible. Gilian, is it really you?"

"Aye, Kappa, it is. You don't know how good it is to see you all again." Gilian dropped the Mevolen accent.

Gliese's eyes widened in surprise and pleasure. "Gilian!"

"We thought you..." Ankaa's voice trailed off in stunned disbelief.

"I know. But I couldn't get news to you that I was alive."

A sudden thought struck Wurren. "Why didn't you tell me in the first place?" he demanded.

"I didn't want attention drawn to me, or else my help would be useless. And..." Gilian rubbed the back of his neck as a sheepish smile crossed his face. "I was scared about what you would think of me being in Algol's guard."

Wurren's breath came out in a long whoosh. "You would have saved me a lot of pain and worry. But what is done is done."

"Am I missing something here?" Vela asked, frowning.

Ankaa grinned at the baffled apprentice. "I forgot. You haven't met Gilian."

Wurren placed an arm on Gilian's shoulder and smiled at Vela. "This is Gilian, my younger brother. He was our last apprentice, the one before Commodore Louris assigned you to us. Gilian, this is Vela, our newest apprentice." He chuckled. "By law, I suppose you're still our apprentice, as well."

The young man bowed low. "Pleasure to meet you, Vela."

"But how are you alive?" Kappa asked incredulously.

"As you probably guessed, I was ambushed by a war band. They hit my horse, and I was thrown against a tree when he thrashed around." Gilian flinched at the painful memory. "Got a bloody arrow in my arm too. But right before they caught me, I threw my chain away. I didn't want them to know I was a Phoenix because, well, we're not supposed to exist."

Kappa laughed. "True enough, lad." He motioned Gilian to continue.

"Algol considered how young I was and forced me to join the army. Later, I made it into his personal guard. That's why I was included on the mission to capture the mysterious Watchman captain who kept messing up Algol's plans." Gilian winked at Wurren. "After they put him in Camp Twelve, Algol sent a few of his personal guards to watch him."

"All that said and done, we should probably introduce you to our friends." Kappa turned to where Deyan was waving him over.

"Aye," Wurren agreed and followed his lieutenant. "We need to talk over a few things."

Gilian moved to follow his brother but then paused and turned to face Vela. "You're not Vela, daughter of Telar, are you?"

"I am," she answered, startled. How could this young, thought-dead Phoenix Watchman know anything about her or her parents?

"I'm sorry about your parents." He took a breath as if to say something more but then clamped his jaw shut.

"Gilian!" Wurren called. "Over here."

"On my way." Gilian bowed to Vela and walked away.

"That was strange." Ankaa stepped up next to Vela. She gave her an accusing look. "You never told me your father was Telar the Great."

"Aye, I'm sorry. I learned very quickly in life that you don't go around blabbing your lineage to everyone you meet." She shrugged. "You would have found out sooner or later, like you just did. But how did Gilian know me and that my parents are dead?"

Across the clearing, Kappa introduced Wurren to the Mevolen ex-soldiers. "Deyan, this is my captain."

The two men clasped arms. "I appreciate that you helped out," Wurren said.

Kappa muttered something under his breath and Deyan smirked. "Pleased to meet you. I've heard a lot about you from your team." He nodded at the other ex-soldiers. "This is Rena, her brother Ralen, Alek, and Heplar. Kappa's probably already told you everything."

"Aye, most of your story I think. So why did you leave the army?"

Ralen stepped up to tell the story. "When we heard Algol was planning to attack Asteri in the next few years, I decided to quit the army to protect Rena. Alek joined us when nothing else exciting happened and we met up with Deyan and Heplar along the way. We have been attacking war bands ever since."

Wurren smiled. "I owe you my life and am glad to have such brave friends." In spite of his welcome, a warning flickered in his head to keep an eye on them.

Lider walked up just then. "No casualties today." He seemed pleased. "Everything went as planned."

"Lider, this is our captain, Wurren." Kappa introduced the two.

"You are the leader of the resistance fighters?" Wurren queried.

"Aye, that I am. Pleasure to meet you."

"And to you," the captain returned the greeting.

"Gilian." Wurren turned to his brother and abruptly changed the subject. "I recall making a promise to help you rescue someone from Algol's castle. What's the situation?"

Gilian glanced at Vela, who had just joined the circle. He did not look eager to share.

"Does it have something to do with these?" Vela held up one of the letters Louris had given them.

Gilian's eyes widened. "How'd you—" He broke off and nodded. "Aye. I should've known that's why you also came."

"How could I have been so blind?" Wurren exclaimed as the two ends connected. *"You're* the informant!"

"Aye, but not the only one. There's a young slave girl, a maid in the castle for Algol's fiancée. The slave acquires most of the information that I send. Her name is"—he glanced at Vela. "Tela."

Vela's face grew white, and she gasped. "Are you sure?"

Wurren reached out to steady his apprentice. She looked ready to faint. "Take it easy," he advised softly.

"Aye," Gilian assured her. "She mentioned you often. Someone else is also in there, one whom I would like to get out too."

"My sister is alive," Vela whispered, her voice barely audible.

"We have to free Tela," Gilian insisted. "I don't know how long it will take Algol to figure out who's been betraying his plans. But when he does…" His voice trailed off.

"That was our mission," Ankaa said.

Wurren nodded in agreement. "Aye."

"Mission? What mission?" Gliese and Kappa chorused with confused expressions.

"Commodore Louris tasked us with finding the source giving us the information and bringing them back to Asteri," Vela filled them in.

Wurren turned thoughtful. "Exactly how will we penetrate Algol's fortress?"

The Watchmen fell silent, clearly uncertain how to answer their captain.

"You won't be able to form a plan until you see the castle," Gilian said. "I spent most of my time inside, so I know the fortress well. Let's camp near the castle and make our plans. They won't expect us to head that way. I know a perfect hiding spot, but it can't hold a lot of people comfortably."

"Good." Wurren nodded, thinking hard. "What do with the other prisoners we rescued? They can't come with us."

The Watchmen glanced over to where the ex-prisoners lay sleeping.

"I will take them back to the forest and look after them," Lider offered.

"That's very kind," Wurren replied. "However, many may wish to return to Asteri. Would you mind escorting them back?"

"I can do that. Or"—he smiled—"Some could join me and my fighters if they wanted to become part of the resistance."

Wurren nodded his approval. "Ask them and see what they say." As always, Wurren was planning ahead, and the ghosts of several ideas popped into his head. "So, the six Phoenix members are going on this mission. Hmm, you didn't happen to bring Twilight along, did you?"

"Um, Wurren?" Kappa shifted, clearly nervous about something.

"Aye?"

"We brought Twilight, but Deyan and his team will most likely be coming along with us."

Wurren's eyebrows rose. "Really?"

"Aye, really." Kappa nodded. "When I tried to exclude them from your rescue mission, Deyan...well...he quoted the Prince against me."

"Hmm. I'll have to remember that." Inwardly, Wurren was laughing. *A Mevolen beat Kappa by using a quote of the Prince. Ha! I'll never let him live this down.*

Later that night, Wurren confronted Deyan and his friends. "I'm sorry to disappoint you, Deyan, but you won't be coming with us to the castle. I want you to stay here with the others."

"You might be a Watchman captain, sir, but you are not *our* commander. You need the help, and we are here to give it. Doesn't your Watchmen oath mention something about never abandoning a friend in time of need?"

Deyan's vast knowledge of Asteri was starting to make Wurren suspicious. Regular soldiers didn't usually know so much about Asteri. *Deyan seems to be an exception,* he mused.

"Aye, but that oath is for Watchmen, and you are not from the League. I may not be your captain. However, I am the commander of this rescue mission." He paused then asked. "How do you know so much about Asteri?"

"We've lived near Asteri for a year and are used to crossing the border for much-needed supplies. We picked up things here and there."

"Kappa was right when he said you were stubborn." Wurren was tired and needed rest, not an argument. "I'll consider it. Do all of you know your weapons well?"

Deyan nodded. "Aye."

"Rena, can you fight, or do you prefer not fighting at all?"

She shrugged. "I'll fight if I must."

"What are you best at?" the captain asked the young woman.

"Blowpipe." She held up her hollowed staff.

The captain turned away. *What am I supposed to do? I am responsible for all who go on this mission, and I don't* want anyone to get hurt. But they can speak Meveli. Only Kappa, Gilian, and I know how to speak it. They could be helpful.

As he walked back to the Phoenix team, his head was crowded with decisions and new thoughts. "Kappa seems to have softened up to Vela," Wurren muttered, watching the two run through a sword drill.

A short distance away, Gilian was fighting Gliese. Wurren had to admit that Gilian had improved greatly. He almost had Gliese for a second, but a swift twist saved the other Watchman.

"What have you decided, Captain?" Kappa asked, turning at Wurren's approach.

Vela struck at the back of Kappa's leg with the flat of her blade, but Kappa casually moved his sword behind his back to deflect the blow.

"Hard choice. They are some of the only people who speak Meveli." He sat down next to his lieutenant.

"Vela speaks it," his friend replied.

Wurren glanced up at his young apprentice. "You do? Why didn't you tell me?"

"I don't know. No need, I guess." Vela motioned across camp. "But the Mevolens are always helpful, and they know a lot too."

"So I've heard." Wurren rubbed his eyes.

"Are you all right, Wurren?" Kappa looked concerned.

"I'll be fine after a good night's sleep." The captain rose and moved off with his thoughts still whirling.

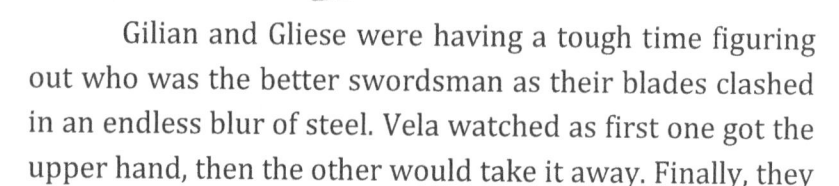

Gilian and Gliese were having a tough time figuring out who was the better swordsman as their blades clashed in an endless blur of steel. Vela watched as first one got the upper hand, then the other would take it away. Finally, they called it a draw and disengaged their blades.

Kappa and Ankaa stood to take their places in the drawn-out circle for sparring, while Gilian sat down next to Vela. "Did the team behave while I was gone?" he asked.

"Mostly. It was a little hard at first because they still missed you," Vela said. "But when Algol took Wurren away, Kappa and Gliese finally started to accept me. We left the base in the hands of other Watchmen," Vela explained.

"What team were you in before you were transferred?"

Gilian certainly had lots of questions, Vela mused. "The Sails."

He whistled softly. "From water to land So, everything was strange at first?"

"You got that right. I didn't even know how to ride a horse." Vela shifted her gaze to the two sparring Watchmen.

"They are a great team once you get to know them," Gilian said. "What was it like on the sea?"

Vela smiled at his many questions, but she didn't mind answering them. "Hard sometimes. As a child, I couldn't run around much because of the small spaces. At night when the sea is calm, it rocks you to sleep and when it's stormy it tosses you about. My favorite thing to do right before the sun sets was to climb to the crow's nest and watch the beautiful colors fade on the water. Of course, we always ran the risk of being caught by the Mevolens. I loved the danger, but one day that all was changed." She stared into the distance.

"I'm sorry."

Vela shook her head. "Don't be. You can't change it."

Ankaa did a bind on Kappa's sword which flew out of his hand. "Rest your arm," she shouted at her opponent. Then Alek challenged Gilian to an archery match and he accepted, leaving Vela to her thoughts.

Ever since I've joined the team, an aching wound has opened in my heart. Will it ever be healed? I wish I had more good times with my parents. All I have in my head is their murders.

Vela's thoughts drifted to her sister, and a twinge of excitement sent chills up her neck. *What will it be like to see Tela again? I wonder in what ways she has changed. Will she remember me?*

Chapter Fourteen

A small figure waited inside the dark shadows, watching. From her shoulders hung a tattered dress that had served her since her capture. She fingered a rip in the hem. *Oh Gilian! Why did you have to get captured? Lord Algol was furious! At least there's no guards at his study.*

She struggled a bit before the lock sprung open. She quietly pushed it open and slid inside the room. Closing the door and stuffing her outer cloak in the crack between the door and the floor, she lit a candle and padded up to the desk.

Taking a sheet of thin paper, the girl traced the maps and copied lists of men, supplies, ships, horses, and weapons. The list included the places where Algol would acquire everything. She could barely read in the sparse lighting but hoped these were the right plans. Stuffing the papers inside her wide belt, she grabbed her cloak and opened the door.

Ten paces down the hallway a voice stopped her. "You there, servant girl."

She turned to find a guard walking briskly towards her. "Aye, sir?"

"What are you doing up at this hour? You wretches know the punishment for sneaking food from the kitchen."

She must think of a plausible lie, and fast. "I needed to—"

"Oh, never mind." He waved her away. "Get out of here."

The servant girl was happy to escape the guard's presence, but another voice froze her flight, and her blood.

"Aren't you one of Mietta's maids?"

Algol! She made a deep curtsy. "Aye, sire." She fixed her gaze on the cold floor next to the lord's feet and she waited.

"You shouldn't be up this late. Get to bed."

She scampered away from the lord, but in her haste, bumped into a guard standing nearby. The papers flew from her belt and fluttered to the stone floor.

"What's this?" Algol stooped and picked up one of the papers.

It took only a heartbeat to decide. The servant girl snatched the rest of the papers and ran. Shouts echoed behind her as she darted through the passageways. The guards were catching up.

Glancing around wildly, she spotted some drapes that covered a doorway. From this hiding place, she heard the guards clatter past. When she thought the coast was clear, she left her refuge and started down the hallway in the opposite direction.

Algol stood in her path. "Just a maid?" His voice was cold and hard. He grabbed her.

She screamed. Not just any scream, but an ear-splitting scream that echoed through the castle and outward, into the surrounding lands.

Gilian sprang to his feet as the rest of the group slowly awoke. "It's Tela! She's been caught!"

"How do you know for sure?" Lider asked skeptically, arching an eyebrow.

"I heard that scream when she and several friends were once chased by a wolf and told her to repeat it if she ever got caught. We must get her out of there!"

"Oh no! What will we do?" Vela's voice was laced in panic.

"We can't do anything tonight," Wurren told her. "Let's get some rest and make our plans in the morning." Wurren turned to Gilian. "You too." His brother and Vela looked ready to take on the Mevolen army by themselves.

"Aye, Wurren," both apprentices agreed through gritted teeth.

Wurren lay awake that night. Too much kept going through his mind to allow him to sleep. *I hope Tela is all right. Would Algol really hurt a young girl?* Across the clearing where the girls slept, Wurren spotted Vela sitting up on her blanket. She was splitting a blade of grass while staring at nothing. *She's probably worried sick.*

The next morning over breakfast, Wurren gathered the group together to make their plans. It wasn't hard to notice that Vela and Gilian didn't eat anything.

"We need one or two people to pose as servants," Wurren said. "They must speak Meveli in case they get separated. Gliese, Ankaa, and I can't go. Neither can Deyan, Ralen, Alek, or Heplar. So, it must be Kappa, Vela, or Rena."

"I speak Meveli," Gilian said. "I want to—"

"You would be recognized and caught right away." Wurren shook his head. "You are a danger to yourself and to Tela if you go."

Gilian closed his mouth but looked crestfallen. However, it was clear he could not argue with the facts.

Wurren summed up the choices then eliminated Rena. "I'm sure Ralen wouldn't want his sister to go in, so it'll have to be Kappa and Vela." The two Watchmen stood before him. "Are you up to the task? I assume Lord Algol has not seen your face. Correct, Kappa?"

Kappa nodded. "I'm always ready, and Algol hasn't seen my face, just a couple lower officers."

"Aye, sir," Vela said. "I too am ready."

"Lider, do you have clothes they could use?"

"We could find them somewhere." The resistance captain went off to find the clothes as Kappa checked the weapons they would carry.

Wurren put Kappa in charge of the mission. He oversaw the weapons he and Vela would carry. "It's simple," he told her. "A dagger per person, and it will be concealed in our clothes or boots."

"But how do we get in?" queried Vela.

Gilian perked up. "That's where I can help! I know all the ins and outs of that castle. One of the perks of being a personal guard meant I toured the dark passages that only they use. I can get you in easily."

"Perfect," Wurren said. "And just as a precaution, if anyone gets seen and captured beforehand, keep on the plan."

Later, Wurren crouched next to the river to get a drink. "We'll be leaving soon for the castle. I hope everything goes well," he murmured cupping his hands in the cool water.

As he stood, his foot slipped on the wet rocks. He regained his balance and turned to go when he heard a cry. A man was being swept down river by the strong undercurrent, his arms flailing wildly to stay afloat. The turbulent waters pulled at the man, trying to suck him under. His head disappeared for a moment before bobbing to the surface.

"Hold on! I'm coming!" Wurren glanced around and spotted a long, sturdy tree branch. Grasping it, he swung it around and held it over the raging waters. The man slammed into the branch, almost wrenching it from the captain's hands. Slowly, Wurren pulled him in until the man collapsed on dry land.

"That was a close call." Wurren knelt and gave to the man his hand.

"Thank you. You saved me." His voice held the twinge of an accent, but it was not Mevolen.

"I'm glad I got to you in time. Where are you from?"

"Yonder castle."

Wurren stiffened then relaxed. The man's clothes were too ragged to be a guard or anyone important. *He's probably a servant or slave.* He stood. "I can take you partway back. You don't look too good."

"Thank you kindly. My name is Beren."

Wurren turned towards the edge of the forest, and Beren stumbled. Catching him, he supported his new companion to the roadside. "You should be able to find your way back from here."

Beren nodded and took a few unsteady steps then put a hand to his head and closed his eyes.

"On second thought, maybe helping you a little farther won't hurt," Wurren said.

As they continued next to the dirt road, the clip-clop of horses' hooves fell on Wurren's ears. "I need to go now, Beren." He loosened the man's grasp from his shoulder.

"No. Don't leave me here." The man's cry made Wurren wince as the horses' gait quickened.

Just then, a score of mounted Mevolen soldiers came into view. Shouting, the warriors charged as they recognized Wurren.

"Beren, run!" Wurren yelled, but the man stood there as if paralyzed.

Drawing his sword, the young captain prepared to defend them both. A warrior rode by, snatched Beren, and swung him up behind him.

Wurren was surrounded. "You'll get a fight out of me this time." He tightened his grip on his sword.

"What about your friend?" a warrior shouted.

Beren gulped as a knife hovered close to his throat. His eyes widened and pleaded with the young man to do something.

In one swift movement, Wurren sent a knife slicing into the shoulder of the warrior in front of Beren. "Help me up on the horse, Beren."

Once again, Beren seemed paralyzed by fear, so Wurren turned to face the warriors again. Several had leveled crossbows at him.

I'm outnumbered. Well, this isn't a first. But I don't want to get captured—

Searing pain flamed across Wurren's back as glass-littered strips of leather dug into his back. He felt blood soaking his cloak and growled in anger. *Second cloak ruined in two weeks. I really need to stop ruining these things.*

The warrior tried again with his whip, but the Watchman was ready this time. He blocked the blow with his sword, simultaneously cutting off half of the wicked whip. Another blow came from behind and something hit Wurren's head. Dazed, Wurren collapsed. Helpless, he was tied and carried back to the castle.

Footsteps echoed down the hall, and two guards straightened when Algol came into view. He passed them without a glance and descended the stairway. Another guard stood as Algol entered the dungeon. He stormed by him and waited impatiently as the guard fumbled for his keys.

Opening the heavy wooden door, Algol stepped into the small cell. The occupant shrank away as he approached. Seizing her by the throat, the Mevolen lifted her small frame into the air and slammed her against the wall. "Who sent you here, Tela?" he growled. "It must've been a good set up if it was planned before I took you."

"N-nobody." Tela gasped for air as his death grip tightened. She squeaked, "I made the choice."

"The *wrong* choice." Disgusted, Algol threw the girl back into the corner. "You really thought you could take my plans?"

Tela's chest heaved up and down, replenishing her air supply. She fingered the marks on her throat and slumped against the wall.

When Tela didn't answer, Lord Algol frowned and slammed the door shut behind him, plunging the room into darkness.

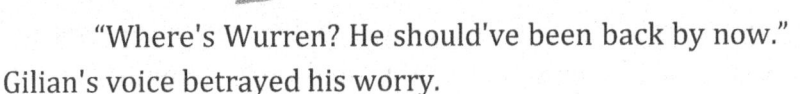

"Where's Wurren? He should've been back by now." Gilian's voice betrayed his worry.

"I'm sure he is fine." But even Kappa looked a little worried. "If he's not back by the time we leave, we will have to go without him."

"We can't go without him!" Vela put in.

"We might have to. He said to go anyway." Deyan leaned against a tree.

Vela glared at Deyan but said nothing.

Late that afternoon, the team, minus Wurren, crept within several hundred yards of the castle. It loomed dark and foreboding in the semi-darkness, and Vela shivered.

Gilian led the group to a rock formation. They climbed to the top and dropped into a black crevice hidden by the shadows. The group waited in complete darkness until Alek lit two torches he had brought. No sound was heard as they moved down the passageway towards the castle.

Splash! Ankaa stepped in a pool of green, stagnant water. She made a face before glancing at the walls. Beside her, Vela ran her hand over the dirt wall. It was damp, and the taller people kept brushing cobwebs out of their faces. No one spoke, and every tiny sound they made seemed amplified tenfold in the tunnel.

Gilian whispered directions to Kappa and Vela when they reached the end of the tunnel, and they slipped out. The passageway had landed them behind the stables near the servants' door.

Kappa motioned Vela to follow him, and together they darted through the rain into the castle. Sputtering torches sat in niches in the cold stone walls. A young servant boy passed them, struggling with the bags he was carrying.

"Let us help you with that," Vela offered in Meveli. She took one of the bags while Kappa took the other.

"Much obliged. I'm taking this food and water to the prisoners." Unlike most servants that Vela had observed, his speech was less coarse and more refined.

"We can take it there if you point us in the right direction," Kappa offered in the same language.

"Thanks. Just head down this hall till the end. You'll see a dark stairway leading into the floor. Make sure to tell the guards by the door that you have the prisoners' meal. They should let you in. Thanks again!"

The boy ran off, and the Watchmen turned to complete their mission. Tapestries on the walls gave a feeling of warmth to the castle, but something about it still made chills go up Vela's spine.

Just as the boy said, two guards stood near the stairway at the end of the hall. One of them leveled his spear at the intruders. "Where do you think you're going?" he asked roughly.

"F-food for the prisoners," Vela stammered.

"Let 'em through, Tethys. They have the bags," the other guard chided.

The gruff guard reluctantly lifted his spear tip. "Get on with it then," he growled, looking suspiciously at Kappa. "Hold on a minute."

Vela glanced back to see Kappa barely avoid the sharp point of the guard's lowered spear by stepping backwards. "You're too old to be a slave. You should be in the army."

Kappa kept his eyes on the floor and didn't respond. The guard's face grew darker.

Vela jumped in. "Sir, he can't speak. They didn't want 'im in the army. He is unstable in the mind, as well." She tapped her head with her free hand and spoke more coarsely than her normal speech. "That's why they assigned 'im to me."

Understanding dawned on Tethys's face and he let Kappa pass.

The two Watchmen hurried down the stairs with their heads bowed.

"Daft?" Kappa muttered. "Do you really think of me like that?"

Vela regarded Kappa with a frown. She was about to tell him otherwise when she saw a smile on his face. She chuckled. "It was the only thing that came to mind."

A horrible stench greeted them, and Vela gagged. *How can the prisoners live down here?* Her companion's face wrinkled in disgust, then turned expressionless.

The stairs curved around and around, and it got darker and creepier. Fewer torches lined the walls, and those that did threatened to go out at any moment. The stairway ended abruptly.

At their footsteps, a guard jumped up from where he was sitting slouched in a chair. "Oh, just servants." He stretched and sat down. "Hurry up and get out of here."

Moving quickly, they walked towards the nearest cell but then changed course. With a swift blow to the jaw, Kappa took the guard out. Vela scooped up his keys. The iron felt cold against her fingers.

One by one, they opened the wooden doors and gave the prisoners food, but Vela saw no sign of Tela. Finally the last cell rewarded their search. At first sight, the cell looked empty except for a mound of rags in the corner. But a dirty face looked up from the mound a few seconds after the door swung open.

"Please don't scream. We heard you last night a mile away," Kappa warned.

"Tela?" Vela said softly.

"Aye?" the girl replied warily, sitting up.

"We're here to get you out. Gilian is with us, but not inside the castle. Come on." Vela extended a hand towards her sister.

"You could be setting a trap so you can kill me," the frightened girl whispered.

"Tela, It's me! Your sister, Vela!" She threw her loose hair over her shoulder to show her face better.

"Vela?" Tela sprang up and they embraced.

"It's nice that you're having a family reunion, but we need to go. *Now.*" Kappa waved for them to follow him.

Chapter Fifteen

"My lord," a guard addressed Algol. "Your spy Beren and Janus's squadron have brought in the important escaped prisoner from Camp Twelve."

"Good." Algol narrowed his eyes. "Why are you nervous?"

The guard looked uncomfortable. "Beren is having second thoughts."

"Hmm." Lord Algol dismissed the guard and strode up the stairs to his council chambers. *Sometimes it's funny when my guards fear me. Then sometimes it's just down-right annoying.*

Beren sat at a table. Nearby, two guards held the prisoner. His head drooped and he was covered in bruises. His cloak was torn and splattered in blood.

"I hear you are having second thoughts, Beren. If you turn him in willingly, you'll get a lot of money. There's been a price on his head since he escaped." Algol gave his spy a scornful look. "If you didn't want to turn him in, you shouldn't have brought him here."

Beren glanced at Wurren from the corner of his eyes. "He saved my life at the river crossing."

"He can't be your friend, you fool. He's from Asteri. They think they're better than us." A twinge of jealousy and hate spiraled up Algol's spine.

A hard look crossed Beren's face and he nodded.

At Algol's command, the guards dragged Wurren out of the room and down the hall. Once out of sight from the

Mevolens, a scuffle broke out. Algol and Beren glanced out the door to see the young captain running down the hallway. His guards lay unconscious on the floor.

Rage filled Lord Algol. "He's getting away!"

Sprinting up the steps, Vela dimly remembered Kappa drawing his knife to deal with his guard. She was too busy knocking out the guard on her side. A shout from Kappa's guard startled her, then it was over.

"It feels like it's taking hours to reach that door," Tela murmured.

As they stepped outside, Vela's feet squelched in the mud. *Great. It stopped raining but there's mud everywhere.*

An alarm sounded as they crossed to the stables. The secret door opened and Gilian jumped out. He caught Tela up and carried her inside the tunnel. Guards were running towards them from all sides. The Phoenix team and Deyan's team ran out to help the two infiltrators. Ralen tossed Kappa his sword and a dirk, while Ankaa handed Vela her sword.

"Deyan!" Kappa ordered. "Someone's coming from the back. Can you cover that?"

"Sure. Wait, is that Wurren?"

"Wurren?" Vela jerked around.

"Did I miss anything?" Wurren asked, running up from behind.

"What happened to your cloak?" Ankaa asked. "And your face?"

Vela followed her gaze to the blood-stained rips on his back.

"Just a scratch."

"Here." Kappa tossed Wurren his sword and drew some arrows just as Algol came out of the keep.

"So, we meet again." The dark lord drew a long sword. "And you brought some friends with you this time too."

"Don't answer him," warned Wurren.

"Deyan."

Deyan's face went white when Algol called his name.

You were such an aspiring young general," Algol said. "Too bad it was ruined. I suppose you never told the Watchmen how you were a spy for three years in Asteri."

Deyan stepped forward and waved the others back. "You all go. I'll stall him. Hurry!"

"We're not leaving without you," Ralen announced.

"Algol wants *me*. I'm your commanding officer and I'm telling you to go!" the young man ordered.

"You betrayed me," Algol growled from behind his helmet. Hate filled his voice.

"You're a poor excuse for a leader. I'll never serve you even if it was the last option on earth." Eyes blazing, Deyan stood ready to fight.

With a cry of rage, Algol attacked the young man with a vicious overhand strike. Out of the corner of her eye, Vela saw Ankaa put a restraining hand on Ralen's shoulder as the young Mevolen tried to join Deyan.

"It's his fight. Leave him to it."

Deyan was a good swordsman; the Watchmen could give him that. But sadly, it was rather obvious to Vela that young Deyan was outmatched.

Deyan fought back with all his strength and nearly got the upper hand once. Finally, a full-force blow from Algol sheared Deyan's sword in two. Instead of retreating, the young Mevolen stood his ground. The sword plunged towards Deyan.

"No!" Rena screamed.

The Phoenix team rushed forward, driving Algol back as Deyan fell into Alek's and Ralen's arms. A deep, red stain was spreading quickly from his chest. Rena jerked her cloak off and tore it into strips to bind the gaping hole in his chest. Algol's sword had gone clean through the young man.

Keep your eyes forward and you don't have to see the blood. Keep looking forward.

Vela repeated it over and over as she stood a few paces from Algol.

He cocked his head at her, inspecting her. "We meet again, little cousin."

Ice froze Vela's veins. "What?"

"I had to prove myself worthy of the throne. Even a half-breed has a right to the throne of Mevol. Killing Telar the Great and his wife was just the thing." Algol scrutinized his reflection on his bloody sword and explained. "Taking Tela and you captive? That worked even better. But those accursed Watchmen had to interfere. I barely managed to escape to the other ship in time."

"No." Vela shook her head. "You must be mistaken. I have no cousins."

"Your foolish mother had a sister. She ignored all advice to marry a Mevolen officer. They had a son, and here I am."

He gave Vela a half bow and pulled off his helmet. A scar ran from his left eyebrow to his ear, and his blue eyes held a mocking look. His blonde hair was slightly curled and hung long, framing his handsome but evil face.

"Y-you murdered my parents?" Vela stuttered. "Does the throne mean so much to you that you would kill your own family to prove yourself?"

"It's easier than you might think."

A hand fell on Vela's shoulder, and she turned to see Wurren. "We can't take him on here. Let's go." Wurren tightened his grip, preventing Vela from launching herself at Algol. "That's an order."

As if in a trance, Vela watched Gliese and Alek carry Deyan into the tunnel. A blur of colors flashed across the scene.

Then she collapsed.

Next thing Vela knew, she was back in the forest, propped upright against a tree. It was morning, and Ralen sat a pace away staring at something.

"What happened?" she asked.

Ralen jerked in surprise at her voice and turned to her. "You collapsed. Rena said it was because of the shock."

"No. I mean...why do you look like that?"

Ralen's eyes gave her an empty gaze. On a normal day, or even a bad day, his eyes shone with confidence, steadiness, and a touch of humor.

Now, they were sad and uncertain.

"Deyan is not well. He hasn't woken up since last night." Ralen looked at the ground. "He's one of my closest friends. We're almost brothers. He never used the term 'I am your commanding officer' before at me. It was kind of startling when he used it last night. Rena is not sure if he'll wake up at all."

"I'm sorry." They both fell silent.

"You're awake!" Gliese walked up. "Captain wants to see you if you are ready to get up."

"Sure." Vela took his hand and rose.

Wurren, Lider, and Alek were standing under a big tree on the other side of the clearing talking in low voices. They stopped when Gliese and Vela approached.

"Vela, did you really have no idea that Algol is your cousin?" Wurren asked.

A terrible dread filled her heart. *Will they kick me out of the League because of my cousin?* "No." Her gaze flicked between the three men. "I didn't even know my mother had a sister."

"You realize I will have to talk to the commodore about this," Wurren continued.

"Aye. I do." She looked at the ground before raising her eyes to meet his. "I understand."

"You do know that Vela is full Asterian?" Lider asked Wurren. "Her father, Telar, descended from one of the noblest families in the country."

"I want her to stay on my team, but Commodore Louris might have something to say."

"Where's Tela?" Vela glanced around the clearing for her sister.

"Ankaa took her fishing to keep her distracted. You can join them. She was worried about you." Wurren motioned in the direction of the river.

"Thank you, sir."

She left as quickly as she could. *If Tela can stay with me, I won't mind leaving the Watchmen. Well, maybe I would a little. All right, I would miss it a lot.*

Following the sound of rushing water, Vela easily found the river. Tela and Ankaa sat with their feet dangling in the water and their lines trailing.

Tela jumped up and nearly squeezed the breath out of Vela. "I still can't believe you came back for me." She let go and sat down but acted too excited to sit still.

"Of course I came back for you. You're my family. Catch anything yet?" Vela settled onto the ground beside Tela.

Ankaa shook her head. "I'm starting to think there are no fish in this river."

"Will we stay together always?" Tela leaned against her sister.

"I hope so. If I can't stay in the League, then we'll definitely be together." Out of the corner of her eye, Vela saw Ankaa blink quickly and look away.

"Why would you not stay?" Tela asked innocently.

Ankaa and Vela exchanged glances, but neither girl wanted to talk about it.

"Where's Gilian, little sis?" Vela changed the subject.

"He went with Kappa to have guard duty." Tela played with a loose string dangling from her pole.

"We should probably get back to camp," interjected Ankaa.

Throwing away their crude fishing poles, the girls made their way back to camp. Vela lagged behind. *I must face the rest of the team sometime.*

Rena was talking with Kappa. He sat next to the fire, warming himself after coming back from the lookout point. When Rena saw the girls, she hurried over. "Deyan's awake. He might just have a chance."

Joy replaced the anxiousness Vela felt. "Is he going to make it?"

"Ralen's in there now, but Deyan's still very weak. But there's a good chance."

Ralen pushed aside the blanket that had kept him from his best friend like a brick wall. This place reminded him of a makeshift hospital. Everyone had donated something to keep Deyan alive—salves, clean cloths, etc. Several bags lined up near a tree held Rena's supplies, and a small creek ran through one corner.

Deyan lay on a clean cloak in the middle of the small, quiet clearing. *Those pine needles probably aren't too comfortable,* Ralen thought.

Deyan's face was white, and his chest was wrapped in bandages, but his eyes were open. Heplar stood nearby and left as soon as Ralen came near. He nearly ran over to his friend's side. "Deyan, please think twice before you do that again," he admonished.

Deyan smiled. "Maybe I should practice a little more. Did the Phoenix team say anything about my past in your hearing?"

Ralen shook his head and Rena pushed aside the blanket. "It's almost breakfast, Ralen. You should probably get something to eat," she said after checking Deyan's pulse.

"Keep him safe, sis. I'll bring you something to eat."

She nodded as if distracted and waved him away.

The meal was light and joyful. Everyone was delighted at the turn in Deyan's recovery. Gilian and Alek came back from guard duty to eat, and Ralen and Gliese replaced them. Most of Lider's group had taken the rest of the ex-prisoners back to Melarin Forest so there wasn't a large group.

We'll head back to Asteri soon, but not until Deyan heals, Wurren thought.

Later that day, Heplar ran out of Deyan's clearing with bad news. An infection.

"His wound is infected?" Vela asked, horrified.

Heplar nodded, pale.

"There's only one remedy for such an infection," informed Rena. "I don't have the plant, *priscillis malinera*. And it's rare to find anywhere except on the plains of Mevol."

The Phoenix team stepped to the side to talk about the predicament and what they should do about it.

"We finished what we came to do, but he is our friend," Kappa said.

"I think we should help him," agreed Gliese.

Ankaa nodded.

"I don't mind," Gilian put in. "He's a good leader."

Wurren glanced over his shoulder and saw Alek telling Ralen the bad news. Ralen threw the stack of firewood he was holding on the ground and ran a hand through his hair.

They prepared to leave the next day. Wurren instructed Gilian, Tela, and Vela to catch as many fish as they could. Kappa and Ankaa would clean them and hang the fish over a fire to dry.

"He must have that plant in a week or else…" Rena didn't finish, but everyone knew what she meant.

"We'll get it," Wurren promised, swinging up onto Twilight.

The Phoenix team was on the trail the next day. Gilian drew up even with Wurren. "Why do you think Algol let us leave? He isn't exactly the 'oh, you invaded my castle. I'll let you go and never bother you again,' type."

"He probably knows something we don't." Wurren could feel the frown on his face. "That is what worries me."

Chapter Sixteen

Vela studied Rena's sketch of the plant intently while her thoughts played out the journey. *It'll take us three nights to get to the plains, then we must find the plant and bring it back. The others will follow to close the distance if Deyan is good. That's not a lot of time.*

On the third night, the Phoenix team was riding near a river when Kappa pointed to a field not too far away. Small, dark-green plants with bright purple flowers grew in rows as far as Vela could see in the greyish light.

"I thought Rena said the plant doesn't spread fast." Gliese studied the field carefully to make sure it was the correct plant.

"Look." Gilian motioned to a parchment nailed to a fence post. "There's a notice over there on the fence surrounding the field."

Ankaa sighed. "I can't read it. It's in Meveli."

"Makes sense. We're in Mevol," Wurren's younger brother said.

"I can read it." Vela squinted at the parchment. "It says that this property belongs to Lord Algol and will be used for the wounded men in the battle against Asteri. Posted by Algol himself."

"I'm sure Algol won't mind us taking one of his plants," Gilian quipped. "He said it was for the wounded, and Deyan is wounded. But what's this about a battle against Asteri?"

"I guess you're right," Wurren said. "Who will go in?"

"I will." Ankaa stepped towards the fence and Kappa gave her a leg up. Dropping lightly onto the other side, she hurried to the plants and pulled one up, roots and all, putting it in a pouch she wore at her belt.

Gliese muffled an exclamation and jerked his head towards a torch bobbing a hundred yards from Ankaa.

Gruff voices in Meveli carried on the light breeze. "We're guarding *plants*. We didn't do anything that bad. We simply gave Tarkan a dunking in the horse trough."

"That was before we knew he was the commander's nephew," the second man said. "But he didn't have to demote us."

"Agreed. This demotion is worse than expected. Nothing ever happens here."

Vela watched Ankaa melt into the shadows as the rest of the team drew back. Then the moon burst out from behind the clouds, illuminating the whole field. A moonbeam caught the blade of Ankaa's drawn knife.

"What's that?" One of the guards pointed at Ankaa, who started running. "You there! Stop!"

Vela held her breath. *Hurry, Ankaa,* she breathed.

Ankaa ignored the guards. Nearing the fence, she vaulted over it and mounted Valiant.

"I don't know what they're saying, but let's get out of here." Gliese turned his horse and trotted off, followed by the others.

They camped for the night in a sheltered clearing on the other side of the river, far enough away to not get caught. As Kappa lay down to sleep, he sat back up before his head touched the ground. "How will we get back to Asteri? Algol will have the border watched."

Wurren looked thoughtful before answering, "I think we'll cross that bridge when we come to it."

The next morning, the Phoenix team packed up and headed back into the heart of Mevol to meet the others. They had to get that plant to Deyan.

Rena had decided not to move Deyan because of how infected his wound was, and they were still quite close to their previous camping spot. Rena rushed over as they rode into the clearing and gratefully accepted the plant Ankaa offered her. "Thank you," she murmured.

Kappa offered to help Rena with the plant. She nodded before dashing off, with him right on her heels.

The Watchmen took care of their horses, taking off their tack and rubbing them down with handfuls of grass before letting them graze. Later, the team sat or lay on the soft, moss-covered grass with Alek, who told them the few things that had happened while they were gone.

"I went to town for supplies when I heard something bad," said Alek.

Ralen appeared behind Alek just then and told him to take guard duty.

"What was Alek talking about?" Wurren demanded. "He heard something bad in town?"

"Seems like Algol is tired of us bothering him. He's sending his best team to find us. Commander Janus, if I remember correctly. If the soldiers saw you in that field, they'll know where we are or our general area and report to the commander."

"We must prepare a nice, warm welcome for them then," Gliese said with a mischievous grin. "It'll take a little bit for Deyan to gain strength to ride again, though."

Two people stayed on watch every second of the day. Each would cover half of the circle around the camp and make sporadically timed rounds around their half.

Vela watched from the edge of the trees as Rena made a poultice with the leaves of the plant, mashing them to extract the plant's healing juices and mixing it with a tiny bit of water. Kappa placed it on the red, inflamed hole in Deyan's chest and wrapped it in a fresh bandage.

Gradually, the infection was drawn out and Deyan woke up. He was still very weak, but he was recovering. After a week and a half, he could be propped up for a little bit. Needless to say, everyone was happy to see him looking better.

Kappa stared into the flames of the small campfire. The flickers of light sent rays darting in and out of the shadows. He was exhausted but had to stay awake on guard duty. *I'm so tired. At least we got the plant to Deyan in time. That's a relief.*

The Watchman had the strangest sensation that he was being watched. His eyes scanned the perimeter of the camp but he saw nothing. He glanced back over the sleeping bodies and detected nothing.

Kappa had learned to never ignore his sixth sense. *Who is watching me?*

His blue eyes flicked up again and this time caught the gaze of shy Rena. For a moment, their eyes met then glanced away. Kappa rubbed the back of his neck as he pretended to study a shadow near the edge of camp, but her brown eyes observed for a moment more before closing. *That's unnerving.* He shook his head to clear the thoughts that sprang to his mind as he stood to go do his rounds.

One night, a week after Deyan's infection had subsided, Gilian ran quietly into camp. Vela sat up as he shook Wurren awake. "They're here!"

Vela scooted over and nudged Ankaa, who woke the others. Alek was on the other side of camp, so Heplar was sent to fetch him. Tela was sent up a tree for safety and Deyan sat in the shadows on the edge of the clearing. He wanted to fight, but Rena prohibited him from even touching his sword.

"Are you sure they came this way, Tethys?" a barely perceptible whisper broke the silence.

"Positive, Commander," came the reply.

Ten men slipped from the shadows and into the clearing. "They're not here," a disappointed voice whispered.

"If Tethys led us here, then they're here, Rhea," the commander's voice was cold.

"Commander Janus." Wurren appeared and stood a few paces from the commander, sword drawn. "We meet again, under better circumstances, I must say."

The Mevolens jumped in surprise. Tethys's shadow muttered a warning while he drew his sword.

"We won't hurt you as long as you don't try to hurt us," Gilian said, coming alongside his brother.

"I should have known you'd turn traitor and go over to the Asterians' side, Gilian," Tethys growled. "Lord Algol will be disappointed."

"Why should he be?" Gilian snapped. "Because I didn't kill my family? Unlike him, I'm not a cold-hearted killer."

Memories flashed before Vela's eyes at Gilian's words, and she tried to blink them away.

"You dare call him that while you are in his country?" Rhea looked shocked in the pre-dawn light.

"I would gladly call him that anywhere," the young man shot back.

"We have a mission, and we won't leave till it's carried out," said Janus.

"Then you might not leave at all," Ralen muttered coldly.

"We'll see about that," another warrior said.

Janus launched himself at Wurren, and his men attacked the rest of the team.

A battle cry rose from the Watchmen and they engaged the enemy.

Vela found herself facing the young woman, Rhea. *Swords aren't my best weapon, but I'll manage.*

The teams seemed well-matched from Vela's viewpoint, even with Deyan not fighting. The group Algol had sent looked like good fighters, unlike most Mevolens, who ran screaming into any fray. These people, on the other hand, fought with swords instead of battle axes. They wielded thin-bladed, curved swords called *talwars* rather than the straight swords of the Asterians.

Next to Vela, Kappa disarmed his opponent. The man retreated, clutching his arm. The rest of the Mevolens closed in to compensate for the gap.

Sudden uncertainty crept up Vela's spine. Rhea had the advantage. She swiped at Vela's chest, throwing the young apprentice backwards as she avoided the blade. The next second, Vela found herself twisted around, with Rhea's knife threatening her throat. Vela grabbed Rhea's knife hand, but her attacker used her other hand to jerk Vela's arm behind her back.

"It'd be so much easier to kill her now," Rhea muttered.

Vela bit back a shriek of pain and panic.

Just then, a flash of metal flew by Vela and a knife hilt struck Rhea full in the face. She yelped and released Vela, who fell backwards. Astonished at her close call, she looked around to figure out what had happened and who had just saved her life. Only steps away, Rhea was still reeling, her hand covering her battered cheek. A look of fury and pain covered her face.

"Get out of there!" Kappa, her rescuer, hollered. He sprang to retrieve his knife and whispered in Vela's ear, "Go sit with Deyan and Rena. "We'll take care of this."

Vela obeyed instantly. She dashed away into the shadows then whirled, intent on watching the battle.

Her heart turned over at the scene. Gliese was having trouble with his opponent, Blafe. The warrior used a long knife instead of a sword. The young Watchman struggled to keep up with the flashing blade, though Gliese was an expert with short blades. He parried again and again, but another knife appeared in the warrior's free hand.

Gilian appeared to be weakening against his opponent's more experienced moves. Tethys's curved blade skimmed Gilian's shoulder, drawing blood.

Vela winced in sympathy. Then her eyes opened wide and she wanted to cheer. With a flash, Gilian's sword retaliated so quickly that Tethys couldn't block the blow. He staggered backwards, blood streaming from a long gash to his sword arm.

A flicker caught Vela's eye from a different quarter. Alek had spotted an opening and lunged. His opponent appeared to let his guard down, and Alek's sword penetrated the warrior's light armor. He gave a cry and fell to his knees. Alek stepped back.

Vela turned her gaze to Ankaa, who looked relaxed. She dodged the blade and dove for her opponent's feet, making him fall backwards. Knocking the talwar from his hand, Ankaa slammed one knee on his chest, her sword tip ending its lunge less than an inch from his chest.

"Your men are mostly wounded, Janus. Give up?" Wurren shouted as he blocked another blow.

"We can't face Lord Algol empty-handed," Janus responded impatiently. "Give us *someone* to take back."

Wurren barked a laugh. "Not likely."

"Commander." Rhea stepped to his side. "We can't win this. Tethys and most of the others are hurt. Only Blafe is uninjured and he's surrounded."

Janus sighed and shrugged. He nodded in obvious defeat before disengaging from the fight. Slowly, he set his sword on the ground in front of Wurren. "Blafe, stand down," he ordered.

Blafe hesitated, then looking around and probably realizing he had no other choice, he set his knives down.

Just then, Rena appeared next to Wurren's shoulder. Her eyes looked worried. "Where's Gliese?"

Chapter Seventeen

Wurren felt his face pale when he realized Gliese was no longer standing with them. In answer to Rena's question, a groan came from across the camp. Wurren darted to where Gliese lay, a pool of blood at his left side. Rena followed at his heels.

After feeling around the wound, Rena sighed in relief before grabbing her bag. "The knife didn't appear to hit any ribs. I think I can get it out. Kappa, could you hold him please?"

Kappa hurried over. He slipped his arms around Gliese's chest and propped him up against his knees. Rena cut away the tunic around the knife wound to give her room.

Wurren bit his lip as he studied Gliese's ashen face, but at least the young man was conscious. *Maybe he'd be better off unconscious,* he mused. He squatted at Gliese's side to wipe away the blood seeping out next to the embedded dagger but accidentally bumped the hilt.

Gliese groaned. "Augh!"

Wurren backed off, feeling worse than ever about his companion.

"Sorry about this, Gliese," Rena warned. "It's going to hurt."

Gliese nodded weakly to Rena and clenched his teeth. "Get on with it."

Rena tugged on the handle, and Gliese reacted with a cry of pain. His hand flew to the hilt, clearly changing his mind about anybody "getting on with it."

Kappa took his hand and gently guided it away. "Come on, Gliese. You can make it," the lieutenant encouraged.

Rena tugged again. Gliese contorted in pain before going limp.

Wurren breathed out his relief. Gliese would feel no pain now that he was unconscious. "Do it quickly, Rena, while he's passed out."

Rena nodded. With one long, steady pull, she dislodged the wicked blade and slid it completely out of Gliese's body. "Quick, a bandage!"

Kappa pressed a folded bandage against the wound to slow the bleeding. A longer strip of cloth was tied around his body, keeping the bandage in place.

"He'll be all right," Kappa reported to Wurren a few minutes later. "The blood flow has slowed. Nothing vital was hit."

"Thank the Creator," Wurren replied. "Any other injuries among the team?"

"Gilian has a slight cut on his shoulder, but that's all. Even Vela didn't get hurt."

"Take care of Gilian while I decide what to do with the Mevolens." Wurren waved a hand at their captives.

"Aye, sir." Kappa motioned to Gilian to approach. He tended on his arm despite the younger man's objections.

Wurren scanned the clearing. The other Watchmen, along with Alek and Ralen, were guarding the disarmed Mevolens. Rhea supported one of the soldiers as best she could. Many of the warriors had wounds, but Rhea's companion looked the worst. He had taken a shallow thrust in his chest by Alek, and it was bleeding profusely. Rhea had torn her jacket into strips to hold against the wound to stop the bleeding, but the blood just kept coming.

"Rena." Wurren beckoned the young woman over. "Can you do anything for this man's wound?"

"Aye, it should be simple. It doesn't look deep."

"Please tend to it then."

Rena nodded and slowly approached Rhea. "I can help with that wound if I may."

Rhea moved to stand in front of her friend. "Not on your life. Why would you help Encel, anyway?"

"Because it's the right thing to do," she replied stoutly.

Encel groaned, and a concerned look crossed Rhea's face. "Okay, but I'll be watching you."

Rena opened her medical bag and went to work.

"Where's Deimos?" Blafe asked, looking around.

"He must have been the one who tried to sneak past us," Rena answered. She pointed at a warrior struggling to rise. "He's over there. Be thankful my dart was dipped only in a sleeping mixture."

Deimos looked around, dazed and shaky. "W-what happened?"

Ralen pointed him towards his friends and nudged him. The warrior slowly stumbled over to his commander with a confused look on his face.

"What will you do with us?" Blafe turned away from Deimos and challenged the Phoenix captain.

Wurren didn't reply. Instead, he turned his back to them and moved across the clearing and into the shadows on the other side. "Deyan? What do you think?"

"Me?" Deyan laughed then pressed a hand to his wound. "Don't make me laugh. It hurts. Why are you asking *me*? You're the experienced captain."

"Aye, but honestly, I have no idea what to do with them. I can't outright kill them, but they can't go back to Algol, either. He'll kill them or make them wish they were dead."

"Hard predicament," Deyan agreed. "Why don't you ask *them* what they want?"

Wurren snapped his fingers. "Good idea, Deyan. Janus has some influence over his men. Thanks. Do you want to come out?"

"Sure. I'm not on the best terms with Rhea, but that's fine." He accepted the proffered hand and stood up. Gritting his teeth against the pain, Deyan, with Wurren's help, walked slowly towards the Mevolens.

Switching to the Rothrias tongue so as not to be understood, Rena exclaimed, "Deyan! What did I tell you?"

"Sorry, Rena. I asked him," Wurren explained.

"No disrespect, sir," Rena scolded, "But aren't you always trying *not* to get anyone killed?"

"Aye, and this short walk won't kill him, I'm certain."

Switching to Meveli, Wurren turned to Janus. "Commander Janus. You know what is best for your men. Do you want to return to Algol or go away somewhere else?"

Vela and Alek gaped at his proposal but held their tongues.

A disbelieving look crossed Janus's face. He narrowed his eyes. "Why are you asking me? Is this a trap?"

"No, it's not a trap. And aye, I'm asking you. What's your choice?"

Janus stood speechless for a moment. Then he spoke. "Nobody ever wants to face Algol when he's angry—"

"I found that out." Wurren rubbed at the bruise that still showed on his face.

Janus looked at his men and shrugged. "We don't want to go back, but where will we go? People like us aren't exactly welcome in Asteri, or in many other places."

"Maybe so. However, we know some people who might be able to help you. They're a band that fights against Algol and the warriors that follow him."

Vela was quietly translating for Ankaa but paused when Kappa turned on Wurren.

"Captain. We can't take them to Lider. What if they're spies?"

"I didn't mean the forest, Kappa," Wurren said. "I meant Deyan and his team. Once he's healed, I assumed they would be returning to their old home. It's not far from us, so we could help them if need be."

Deyan frowned and he leaned against a tree. "I don't know about that, Wurren. We're rebels. They're as high as Algol's personal guard."

"If they join you, then they'll be rebels too," Wurren argued. "Anyway, they could teach you a few things. But don't answer right now. Think about it, talk it over with your group, and tell me your answer tonight."

Deyan nodded.

As the sun rose higher, everyone ate breakfast, and Kappa left to guard the camp. With the number of prisoners, Wurren couldn't afford to send another guard out.

The Mevolen warriors sat in a small group, mostly silent.

After breakfast, Wurren was sitting beside Gliese when he woke. The young man was weak, and pain wracked his face when he moved.

Wurren cringed in sympathy. *I hate to see Gliese in pain. I wish I could do something more for him, but I can't.* He offered him a leather bottle of water. After taking a brief drink, Gliese fell back into a deep sleep.

Deyan limped past Wurren and handed the Mevolens a bottle of water to share. With a dark look, Rhea accepted it and took a brief sip before passing it to Encel, who looked better thanks to Rena's earlier ministrations. Rhea stared at Deyan, who simply looked back at her. Then the two of them moved a few paces away from the others to talk privately.

Wurren had sharp ears. He listened without appearing intrusive.

"You ran away," she accused Deyan.

"I couldn't do it anymore, Rhea. I was done."

"You can't just walk away from your job, from Lord Algol, or from me. We were nearly there, Deyan. You were the best spy Lord Algol had and I was near the top of the squadron. When you disappeared, Lord Algol suspected I was somehow involved and he demoted me." Her eyes flashed.

"I'm sorry, Rhea," Deyan whispered, "But I wasn't comfortable anymore. We couldn't continue like we were doing. I have changed now. The Asterians are kind and noble. They have given us another chance."

She shrugged. "It'll never be the same between us, Deyan. Never."

A little sadly it seemed, Deyan's head dipped once before he painfully moved away.

The day passed uneventfully, and night fell sooner than anyone expected. The captured Mevolens often glanced warily at Deyan, wondering if he had made his decision.

Deyan had talked to his team, and Wurren knew he was ready to reveal his decision. "We have decided to let them stay with us," Deyan said. "We could use their help, but"—he paused—"it's just, can we trust them fully?"

"That's what I'm wondering too," Wurren said. "Algol could have told them to let us capture them, but Janus seems like a good commander. I don't think he would risk losing his men to a trap."

"If you say so."

Wurren relayed Deyan's decision to the Mevolens. Janus looked troubled. "You can't go back to the north, you know. There's an army spread out across Mevol near the border. They'll surround us and capture you."

"So that's their plan," muttered Ralen.

"Could we make it to the sea? We could cross the border by going along the coast." An escape plan was forming in Wurren's head.

"Possibly. But we'd have to move fast. Our horses are tied to a tree a little ways that way." Janus waved back the way they had come.

"Let's go, then. Kappa, make a couple of stretchers for Gliese and Deyan to ride. They're still pretty weak." Wurren turned to Encel. "Can you ride, Encel?"

"Aye."

"Good. Vela, pack up the camp. Ankaa, please saddle your horse and Vela's too."

"Aye, sir," Ankaa replied.

"Alek, find Ralen and relieve him from guard duty. I think we can manage without one."

At the captain's orders, the camp sprang into action.

Wurren found Gliese off to one side and told him of the decision. The young man immediately started protesting, "Do I *have* to ride on a stretcher? I can ride Daga."

Wurren held up a hand to forestall objections. "You will rest on the stretcher. I will not risk you bleeding to death before we get home."

Gliese hung his head and nodded, resigned.

It took half an hour to get ready and organize the marching line, but to Wurren it felt like forever. "Wounded first, accompanied by Heplar, Rena, and Ankaa," he directed. "Janus, you go next. The rest of us will be behind you, watching for anyone following. We'll travel throughout the night and get as far away as possible from here."

And travel all night they did.

By the time morning came, everyone was slouched in their saddles and tired, especially Deyan, Gliese, and Encel, who were weaker than the others. When they made camp that morning, Ralen reported the Mevolen army was moving out of a village several miles away and would overtake this place before sunset. Everyone was tired, hungry, and some were sore.

Grimly, Wurren pushed on.

Chapter Eighteen

They traveled the rest of the day and ended up in the middle of a grassy plain on a hilltop. No fires were allowed, and hardly anyone ate before collapsing on the ground in exhaustion.

Vela's eyes sprang open sometime later, and she gasped, only to relax again. The stars above her were starting to fade in the growing dawn. *I wonder who's on guard duty.* She sat up and glanced around. *Everyone is still asleep. Guess I'll put myself on guard duty.*

Undoing Tela's tight grip on her sleeve and wrapping her cloak snugly around herself, Vela made her way to the bottom of the hill and sat facing north, the direction of the Mevolen army.

A whisper of grass came from behind her. Vela whirled. Kappa was coming to join her. They sat in companionable silence for a few minutes.

"Couldn't sleep?" She started the conversation.

"I couldn't stop thinking how dreadful it would be if someone snuck up on us."

"Same here," Vela said then continued, "Why were you so cold to me when I first came to the cabin?"

Kappa shifted into a more comfortable position. "I guess I was still sad about Gilian. I know that gives me no excuse to treat you like that though. You really do make a great addition to the team...even if you think I'm crazy."

Vela laughed softly at the lighthearted comment. "I understand. I got upset at Muhif several times for not saving

Tela. But I eventually got over it, mostly." She stared at the lightening sky. "When Wurren was taking me to the Command Center, we got to know each other better. He never talked about Gilian, just like I never talked about my sister. We had the same holes in our hearts, only we didn't know it."

"Gilian's was like a younger brother to all of us," Kappa said, "So we took it hard. He cracked jokes when we were still tense from a raid. He made every job more fun by making lighthearted comments at random times. We missed him." Then Kappa changed the subject. "I must say, I didn't really think Janus's patrol would still be here."

"Me neither. It seems odd. I think they were as exhausted as we were." Vela glanced at Kappa and glanced away quickly when she caught him looking at her.

"I do hope you will stay with the Phoenix team," he said.

"Aye. But what will happen to Tela? She can't stay with us in the cabin, and I won't leave her by herself. I've been trying to think of a solution, but nothing has come to mind."

"I don't know. Let's worry about getting back to Asteri first."

Vela smiled and nodded.

As they watched, the sky began changing before their very eyes. The dark blue turned to purple, then pink, orange, and then to yellow. A lark flew by, announcing the arrival of dawn. It swooped through the air looking for grubs to eat.

Finally, the sun leaped up from behind a hill, bathing the whole plain in golden rays.

Behind them, Vela heard a few movements from the other sleepy travelers as they awoke to start the day.

"You go on back. I'll stay on watch." Kappa stood and helped Vela to her feet.

She nodded and went up the slope. Looking back once, Vela saw the lone figure still standing, gazing over the plain, oblivious to the wind tugging at his cloak. *We'll all fight to the last man, that's for certain. I just hope it doesn't come to that.*

Back at camp, only Rhea and Blafe had awakened. Tela was still sleeping peacefully next to where Vela had lain, her hand resting on Vela's bed. Wurren, Deyan, and Gliese were recovering from wounds, so they too were sleeping.

The others were just...tired. Keeping an eye on the Mevolens who were awake, Vela rolled up the blanket she had used for sleeping and pulled out breakfast. It was the same dried fruit and meat as last night's meal. "Good morning," she greeted them quietly.

"Morning," they replied as she passed them the food bags.

Silence fell while they ate. Then Vela asked, "Rhea, back when we were fighting, you said it would be easier to kill me, but you never did kill me. Why not?"

Rhea took a moment to answer. "Lord Algol told us to bring back the girls alive. I don't know why he wanted you and the others. I was just doing my job."

"Probably because Tela and I are his cousins," Vela mumbled, not at all pleased with Algol's hospitality.

"His *cousin*?" Blafe asked in disbelief.

"Aye, but don't think for a second that I enjoy it."

"Well, I answered your question. Now, you answer mine," Rhea challenged. "Why didn't you kill us back when you easily had the chance?"

Vela hesitated and composed her answer before replying, "As you know, most Asterians believe in the Son's words and the Good Book. The Good Book says that we are never to murder. In fact, it is one of the Ten Commands that the Creator gave us to obey. It doesn't mean that we can't defend ourselves. But if, for example, your team was unarmed, it wouldn't be right to kill you. Does that make sense?"

Blafe nodded. "I think it does. I've heard of this Son but never learned a whole lot about Him. He sounds like He would make a good king."

A smile brightened Vela's face. "He is the Prince. His Father is the Creator, the King of the whole world."

For a few minutes Rhea contemplated Vela's words. "I would like to know more about the Son sometime," she finally said. "Could you tell me more once we're out of Mevol?"

Vela nodded with enthusiasm. "I would love to tell you more."

Wurren stood just then. He rolled up his blanket and rubbed the sleep from his eyes. *He's still tired,* Vela noted silently. And why not? The captivity, the fighting, and the traveling were a bad mix for anyone.

"Kappa is on watch, Captain." Vela handed him the food bags.

He nodded his thanks and sat next to her, running a hand through his hair.

Inwardly, Vela laughed. *I wonder if I should tell him that just made his hair worse!*

"I feel terrible that he has to establish a sentry," Wurren admitted. "Normally, that's my job but today—"

"Don't blame yourself, Wurren. We all slept heavily, and you need your rest, especially—" Vela stopped as Tela gave a huge yawn and pulled herself upright.

After everyone woke and ate, they broke camp. It was only an hour's ride to the sea, and everyone was eager to cross into Asteri.

When the group arrived at the shore, the salty air whipped past their faces as they gazed on the waves crashing on the beach. Wurren sent Gilian along the coast to see if the Mevolen army had reached the shore yet.

He came back with dire news. "The army has cut us off at the beach. They must have guessed our plan." He dismounted a little shakily from Daga. "Daga still hasn't gotten used to me. Thanks for letting me ride her though, Gliese."

Gliese nodded. He still looked miffed at not being able to ride his own horse.

"Then we might have to change our plans," Wurren said. "We'll go by sea. Vela, can you captain a ship?"

All the eyes shifted from Wurren to Vela. She squirmed. "Me? But you're the captain and besides, I can't sail a ship. I never finished my training."

"You are the only one among us who has any experience on the sea. You tell us what to do, and we'll do it. First, we will need a ship." Wurren turned towards a dock not too far away.

"Don't take a warship," Vela advised. "They're heavy, slow, and unmanageable. If only Mevolen ships are docked, then you'll want the smaller, lighter patrol ships." The words escaped her mouth before she could bite her lip.

Ralen smirked. "It looks like we have a captain."

Before Vela could put together a fitting reply, her attention was drawn to the Phoenix captain, asking her if she saw a patrol ship. Scanning the docked ships, she spotted one ship that perfectly suited their needs and was situated near their position. She pointed. "That one."

The group carefully approached the ship and found it guarded by three Mevolen soldiers. Wurren frowned at this new obstacle.

"Blafe and I can take care of them," Janus whispered to Wurren.

The captain was silent for a moment before answering, "Aye. Just remember, we're watching."

A nod from Janus and he moved off to inform Blafe. A few minutes later, the two Mevolens rode up to the guards. They held a conversation that the Watchmen and their friends could barely hear.

"I'm Commander Janus. We're looking for the group that has been causing a nuisance. You haven't seen them anywhere, have you?" he asked with authority.

"No, sir. We heard that some rebels are on the loose. If they come this way, we'll catch 'em." The guards snapped a salute.

"Good."

Blafe nodded. He turned his horse in an act of leaving, but a stray hoof "accidentally" caught a soldier on his shoulder, sending him flying backwards on the wharf. He fell heavily and lay still. A knife and sword sufficed for the others.

Those soldiers didn't have a chance, Vela thought.

Bounding out from behind some trees, the rest of the fugitives joined Janus and boarded the ship.

Gliese, Deyan, and Encel were taken below as they were the worst casualties. Heplar went with them as a healer, leaving the others to navigate the ship.

Kappa turned to Vela and saluted. "What first, Captain?"

She shoved him. "Don't you start too. I've never set foot on one of these patrol ships before. How am I supposed to know—"

"Vela." Wurren's serious voice stopped her mid-sentence. "I told you that you have the most experience. You grew up on the sea. To be honest, the sea and I don't get along well. I speak for my team when I say none of us have been on the sea for more than two days."

Vela sighed. "I just don't want to get us killed."

"We believe you can do this." Rena laid a hand on Vela's shoulder.

Vela closed her eyes. *Why am I refusing to do the one thing I know how to do? I've been on the sea for most of my life. Oh Creator, help me.*

She straightened. "All right, then. Wurren and Alek, two lines are holding us to the dock. Untie them and coil the ropes. Gilian, Ralen, Blafe, and Kappa, unfurl the sails."

Alek and Wurren jumped to their tasks, but the other four stood confused. "Sorry. I'll help you with that. Follow me." Vela leaped onto the rigging and scampered up like a monkey. The others followed clumsily behind her.

Halfway up, she called down, "Have any of you piloted a ship before?"

One of Janus's team slowly raised his hand. "I have." Deimos said, the man Rena had darted back at the clearing.

"Set our course for farther out to sea," she ordered.

Showing the young men how to unfurl the sails, Vela slid down a rope to adjust the sails. The mizzen sail was crooked. Enlisting the help of Tethys and some of the others, she set it straight and secured the line.

"Perfect!" Ralen said with a smile.

"We're not there yet," Vela said. "We still have quite a way to go." She took the wheel from Deimos, and they were off.

The winds blew fair as they sped northwest. Keeping land in sight, they planned to creep along the Mevol coastline to Asteri and try to dock at a port. Wurren and some of the others were talking below deck about what to do if they were attacked by a Watchmen ship. After all, they were sailing a Mevolen patrol ship.

Vela heard other sounds too. Someone had found the galley and was making a meal. After consulting the maps, she guessed that it would take about six days of straight sailing to make it to the closest Asterian port and that didn't include storms or loss of wind.

It took no time at all before Vela regained her sea legs. She couldn't say the same about the other "sailors." Janus and some of his men looked at home on the water, but the Watchmen looked a little sick.

Chapter Nineteen

Later, Ankaa came out with two plates of food. Giving one to Vela, she leaned against the railing. "I'm glad Commodore Louris sent you to us. I know it might not have seemed like that in the beginning."

"I am thankful too," Vela replied. "You were the first to open up to me. Thanks." They shared a smile. "Do you have your sea legs yet?"

"Aye. How'd you get used to the rocking so fast?"

A smirk spread across Vela's face. "You get used to it after a few years, and then it comes back quickly."

Silence.

"I'm sorry you had to find out about your cousin that way," Ankaa said softly.

Anger and sadness washed over Vela. "No need to apologize. I had to find out sooner or later. I'm just grateful that Tela is safe."

More silence.

Vela glanced at the maps and sighed. "I've never done anything like this before. Oh, I've charted courses and helped with the sails, but sailing my own ship?" She shook her head.

"There's a first time for everything," her friend reminded her.

"Aye, but I get no second chances doing this."

"You won't fail."

A weak, uncertain smile greeted Ankaa's comment.

After Ankaa returned below deck, two figures, well balanced against the roll of the ship's deck, found Vela and asked questions, this time about the Son and the Creator.

Vela smiled her delight and urged them to ask whatever was on their minds.

"If the Creator is perfect and we are sinners," asked Rhea, "How can we ever live with him?"

Adjusting the wheel of the ship to keep it going in on course, Vela answered, "The Good Book says, 'For the Creator so loved the world, that He gave His only begotten Son, that whoever believes in Him shall not perish, but have eternal life. For He did not send the Son into the world to judge the world, but that the world might be saved through Him.' If you just believe that the Son, the Prince of the world, came to earth, died for your sins, then was raised to life on the third day, then you will be able to spend eternity with Him in paradise after you die."

Blafe stroked his chin while he absorbed this information. "I would like to believe in the Prince."

Rhea echoed his statement.

Vela knew her face was glowing at this news. "Then just pray to Him and tell Him that you believe, and He will wipe away all the stains of your sin."

Rhea raised her eyebrows. "It's that simple? I thought it would be something harder."

Vela nodded. "Aye. It's that simple. I can help you if you like."

"I need some more time to think about it," Blafe said. "But thank you for opening our eyes."

They disappeared down the hatch leaving Vela alone. *Creator, please show Rhea and Blafe Your love and guide them in making this decision.*

Three hours later, Deimos came up to give Vela a rest. She gladly turned over the wheel and found a spare bunk. She lay down, exhausted. This job was more draining than anything else she had done before.

Alek shook her awake five hours later.

"What's the matter, Alek?" A million scenarios raced through Vela's head. Not one of them was good.

Alek explained as they hurried up to the deck. "Tethys spotted a ship off to the west where the fog is lighter. Wurren says it flies the Asterian flag. But why would they be in Mevolen waters?"

"I don't know. Are you sure it is Asterian?" A nod confirmed her fears.

Suddenly, a thought struck Vela. "To the west? There is a dangerous rocky reef that way. I wonder if the ship is stuck." She made her way to the side of the boat where the others were gathered.

Where'd this fog come from? It feels like a heavy blanket, and I can't hear any noise the other ship is making. Ugh, it seems to be trying to suck my breath away.

Peering through the heavy fog, she waited till the fog lifted slightly before identifying the ship as Asterian.

"They aren't moving," observed Janus, intently scrutinizing the ship.

"They're stuck. You can see the waves breaking against the rocks near them." After Vela pointed out the problem, everyone saw the trouble. "It's Rebel Reef. One of the most treacherous places in the Rothrian Sea."

"Can we rescue them, Captain?" questioned Encel.

Wurren didn't respond, so Vela elbowed him. "What? Oh, I thought you were talking to Vela. I could get used to her being captain. Is it possible to rescue them, Vela?" He turned the question to the new sea captain.

"If we use the small boat, but they might—"

"Get down!" Rena yelled as a small volley of arrows flew from the other ship. Shouts followed the missiles, and they weren't pleasantries one uses with a neighbor.

"But they might fire at us," Vela finished wryly.

"That was close. How will we convince them we're friends?" Janus asked. "The only way I can think of is a white flag."

"Aye! That's it," Vela agreed. "We can use the small boat and row closer, waving a white flag. Watchmen respect a white flag." Vela dashed off to the captain's quarters to find the right flag. It was dark inside, and the flag box was not in order, but she spotted a scrap of white and jerked it out. Stepping out on the deck, she found the others discussing their rescue plan.

"Who should go?" Kappa asked.

"You Watchmen should go," Alek said. "They probably wouldn't trust any others."

"I'll take Vela, Gilian, and Kappa." Wurren's voice left room for no arguments.

They climbed into the boat, and the crew lowered it into the water. Wurren and Kappa took their places at the oars. Gilian held the flag, which he had attached to a spare oar, and waved it above his head. Vela sat in the stern to guide them.

As he bent forward for another stroke, the Phoenix Captain ducked away from the last arrow. "They're good shots," he commented wryly as the shots stopped.

As they drew closer to the ship, Vela stared at it. *It's a Watchman ship!*

A muscular figure appeared out of the mist on its deck. "We will not surrender!" he cried, waving his sword above his head.

Vela's heart leapt into her throat and nearly choked her. "Muhif!" she shouted. "It's me, Vela! We're here to rescue you."

Muhif froze and the sword dropped from his hand. Then he spun around and bellowed orders at the Watchmen sailors.

Gilian and Kappa moved the rowboat within fifteen yards of the ship. They could go no farther. Waves crashed against the deadly reef on which the ship sat.

Sailors crowded at the rails before splitting into two groups consisting of eight and three men. The group with eight men headed to the emergency rowboat kept at the back of the Watchman ship. Meanwhile, the other few men ran to the side of the boat.

"Do you have room in your boat for three more men?" Muhif called down.

"Aye. That we do," Wurren shouted. "But we can't move any closer. The reef is too dangerous."

Spray coated the Phoenix Watchmen as Kappa and Wurren struggled to hold the boat steady against the constant swells. Vela shielded her eyes from the flying water and watched the three men consult. Then, suddenly, they jumped over the edge of the boat. A loud *splash* accompanied each man as they landed in the water.

Three heads bobbed to the surface before they started swimming towards the boat. But one head lagged behind the other two, his strokes growing slower and slower till he was barely treading water.

"Cook!" Vela shouted. She stripped off her cloak and outer coat before jumping to her feet, setting the boat rocking in violent motions.

Wurren knew what she was going to do before she even moved. "Vela, no!"

But she ignored him and dove into the fridged waters. Muhif blinked in surprise as she swam past him and made it to Cook's side. For a few seconds, both Vela's and Cook's heads went under. Then they appeared again with Vela supporting Cook.

Gilian had a difficult time hauling Cook into the rowboat. Vela gripped the side of the boat as she waited her turn. Water sloshed against the boat side, splashing into her face as her hands slowly grew numb from the cold. Then Gilian had her arm and was dragging her into the boat.

"What did you think you were doing?" Wurren demanded. He heaved at his oar, sending the boat speeding towards their own ship.

"S-saving Cook's life." Vela's teeth chattered.

Shaking his head, Wurren picked up the cloak she had thrown off and tossed it to her, trying to move the oar at the same time. Vela nodded her thanks and wrapped it round her shoulders. Cook sat next to her on the narrow bench and gave her a warm smile of thanks.

Gilian had put Muhif at the other end of the boat and Vela couldn't wait to speak to him. *There's so much we can catch up on!*

Kappa pulled in his oar and grabbed a rope, securing the small boat to the larger one. One by one, they all climbed up the ladder and stumbled onto the top deck. Ankaa snatched up a blanket and wrapped it tightly around Vela's shoulders.

"Are you all right?" Ankaa asked breathlessly. "We saw you jump in from here."

"I-I'm fine." Vela shivered.

Wurren turned on her. "There are other ways to save someone's life that don't include being reckless and jumping in freezing cold water."

"But it wasn't cold for me," Vela protested. "I've been in colder."

"That's not the point—" Wurren stopped and ran a hand through his hair. "I don't want to lose another apprentice—"

"Vela!" Muhif stepped around Wurren and engulfed her in a hug. "I've missed you so much."

"I missed you too," she replied, letting go and smiling at him.

"Now." Muhif turned back to Wurren. "Where's your captain?"

Kappa turned away coughing and Vela caught a glimpse of a smile on his face.

"I am the captain," Wurren said and frowned at his lieutenant, who stopped coughing.

"*You?* Forgive me for saying this, but aren't you a little young?" Muhif questioned.

Muhif still hasn't stopped speaking his mind, thought Vela.

"He is the captain, Muhif," Vela urged.

Deyan limped slowly up to Wurren and said, "The men are fed and are going below for some sleep."

"Thank you, Deyan." The Phoenix captain nodded.

At the name Deyan, Muhif placed a hand on the hilt of his dagger. "You're the spy the commodore warned us about," he growled fixing a dark look on the young man.

Deyan swallowed nervously. "That was several years ago. I've changed."

"Of course, you say that. You're lying." Muhif's grip tightened on his dagger.

Kappa jumped in between the two. "Hold on. Deyan has proven that he can be trusted, and so can the rest of his team. He even took on Algol to buy us time to escape."

Muhif reluctantly let go of his knife. "What about the other Mevolens? You obviously haven't been a captain very long if you let them stay."

It looked like Wurren bit back angry words before replying, "I have been a captain for two years."

"My apologies." Muhif's look did not appear sorry to Vela.

"Why are you and your ship so far into Mevolen waters?" Kappa asked.

"Don't you know?" A shocked look crossed Muhif's face. "Where have you been the past few weeks?"

"In Mevol," Vela answered dryly.

"You didn't hear?"

"Hear what?" Vela demanded.

"Lord Algol has overtaken all of Asteri."

Mia L. Johnson

Watchmen of Asteri Series

Book Two

Coming soon!

Characters:

Algol, Vela's cousin and a murderous varmint

Alek, serious and cautious; drafted into the Mevolen army against his will

Ankaa (*Ann-ka*), Vela's first friend in the Phoenix team; horse Valiant

Beren (*Bee-ren*), spy for Algol

Blafe, special weapons expert with knives

Captain Wurren (*Were-in*), young for a Watchman captain; takes his job seriously; stern at times but has a nice side; horse Twilight

Commodore Louris (*Lor-is*), manages all the Watchman groups across Asteri

Deimos (*Day-mos*), can steer a Mevolen patrol ship; part of Janus's squadron

Deyan (*Day-in*), leader of the small band that harasses the Mevolens any chance they get; previously a spy for Algol

Encel, a soldier under Janus's command

Gilian (*Gill-an*), Wurren's younger brother and a Phoenix apprentice; also used to be one of Algol's personal guards

Gliese (*Gleze*), prankster of the Phoenix team; favorite weapons are knives, fists, and anything else he has on hand; best at anything except a sword and bow; horse Daga

Heplar, Rena's healer helper; first Mevolen the Phoenix team encounters on their journey

Janus, commander of Algol's elite group

Kappa (*Cap-uh*), Phoenix team's lieutenant; rarely smiles but finds delight in playing his violin and scaring the living daylights out of people; best healer in the Phoenix team; horse Dermen

Lider (*Ly-der*), Lider leads the resistance in the Melarin (Me-lar-in) Forest

Ralen (*Ray-len*), brother of Rena and the liveliest of Deyan's band; raised on a farm

Rena (*Ree-na*), specializes in blowpipe and healing; sister of Ralen; raised on a farm

Reng, prisoner in Algol's notorious Camp Twelve

Rhea (*Rea*), swordswoman

Muhif, a Watchman sea captain; incredibly strong; barely smiles; takes orders only from the king and Commodore Louris

Tela (*Teal-a*), younger sister of Vela; spy inside Algol's castle

Telar the Great, wealthy merchant on Rothrian Sea; Vela and Tela's father; deceased

Tethys (*Teth-is*), prison guard; hates Gilian; best tracker in Janus's patrol

Vela (*Veil-uh*), a young apprentice sea Watchmen; transferred to a legendary team in the mountains

Acknowledgements:

I am sure all you readers might be a little mad at me for the rather abrupt ending to this first book, but sometimes we authors are just evil that way. 😊 Please stick around for the rest of the acknowledgments so you can hear about all the amazing people who helped me through this three-year adventure.

There are no words to express my thanks and gratitude to the one who made all this possible. God gave me a gift for words and I hope and pray that I may only use it for spreading His good news.

Special thanks to Annette Engle and Jillian Morrissey. When it came to spelling and grammar checks, you two were on it as fast as lightening. It is wonderful to have friends who can point out every mistake you make. Thank you also for helping me get the wonderful pictures for the front page.

Another thank-you to Lilianna Lazenby, my dear friend. You were my inspiration to keep writing and a constant encouragement throughout the whole lengthy process.

Thanks to my siblings, Evan, and Lily Johnson. Evan, you were one of the first people to read this story (in one of its roughest forms) and were with me all the way. Lily, the hours I spent reading to you and seeing your reactions were some of the best parts of writing this story.

Thank you, Mrs. Marlow, for being my editor. You brought the professionalism to my chaotic writing and I couldn't have done this without you.

And to the final readers, Emery Johnson and Elizabeth Quinsland. Thank you for the final insight and wonderful help looking at the plot line and checking for any final mistakes.

And the last thanks goes to Mr. Jonathan Burley Sr. who told me everything I needed to know from publishing to formatting and everything in between.

Thank you everyone!

Author's Note

Hi, I am Mia Johnson. Thank you so much for reading my book. I have worked with Vela, Wurren and the others for so long they have become real to me. I hope they seemed real to you too, if just for a little while. Please come back for the thrilling sequel.

But now, a little about myself.

I have been raised for most of my life in the green hills of Oregon along with my seven siblings and two awesome parents, where I taught myself archery and started my writing career. I love sketching, country dancing, and music. I am sixteen at the printing of this book and I hope to impact my readers, encouraging them to be chivalrous, kindhearted, and loyal while following God with their whole hearts.

Mia L. Johnson